DATE DUE			

THE SELECTED STORIES
OF
RICHARD BAUSCH

THE SELECTED STORIES
OF
RICHARD BAUSCH

THE MODERN LIBRARY

NEW YORK

1996 Modern Library Edition

The stories which appear in this collection have previously appeared in the
following journals: *The Atlantic Monthly, Esquire, Harpers, The New Yorker,
Redbook,* and *Wigwag.* In addition, they have appeared in the following
collections: *Spirits and Other Stories* (The Linden Press/Simon & Schuster,
1987), *The Fireman's Wife and Other Stories* (The Linden Press/Simon &
Schuster, 1987), and *Rare and Endangered Species* (Houghton Mifflin/Seymour
Lawrence, 1994).

Jacket photograph © 1996 Jerry Bauer

Printed on recycled, acid-free paper.

Library of Congress Cataloging-in-Publication Data is available

ISBN 0-679-60189-9

Manufactured in the United States of America

2 4 6 8 9 7 5 3 1

RICHARD BAUSCH

Richard Bausch was born on April 18, 1945, in Fort Benning, Georgia. He and his identical twin brother, Robert, who is also a novelist, were among the six children of Robert Carl and Helen Simmons Bausch. In 1948 the family moved to Washington, D.C., and two years later they settled in Silver Spring, Maryland. Bausch remembers being raised in a devout Catholic household where the rosary was recited every night: "I believe we learned from that experience that words counted for everything: one could address them to the dark, to the night stars in faith that they could be heard and that they mattered." Another formative experience was his father's storytelling: "I grew up listening to my father tell stories—he is a great storyteller, and all the Bauschs can do it." After finishing high school Bausch served in the U.S. Air Force for four years. After his discharge he briefly toured the South and Midwest with the "Luv'd Ones," a rock band. On May 3, 1969, he married photographer Karen Miller and they soon moved to Fairfax, Virginia, where he enrolled in fiction workshops at George Mason University. After he earned a B.A. in 1974 Bausch entered the creative-writing program at the University of Iowa, studying with John Irving and Vance Bourjaily. He received an M.F.A. in 1975 and returned to teach at George Mason, where he is now the Heritage Professor of Writing. Bausch received the Award in Literature from the American Academy of Arts and Letters. He lives with his wife and five children in rural Virginia.

Real Presence, Bausch's first novel, was published in 1980 to highly favorable reviews. "This is Flannery O'Connor country," said *Time* in praise of this story about the crisis of faith endured by an aging priest in a small Virginia parish. "A unique and stunning performance," hailed James Dickey. In his next novel, *Take Me Back* (1981), which was nominated for a PEN/Faulkner Award, Bausch examined the troubled lives of a hard-drinking insurance salesman and a sixties rock musician who also happen to be husband and wife. "Richard Bausch has captured something essential in the quality of American life today in these pages," wrote *The Washington Post Book World.* The author's third book, *The Last Good Time* (1984), is an astonishingly affecting narrative, by turns funny and disturbing, about the odd-couple friendship between two old widowers. *"The Last Good Time* is the most compassionate view of the modern world that I have ever read," remarked Mary Lee Settle. "Bausch finds grace and joy in the midst of the inevitable and the terrible." And Walker Percy deemed it "a triumph—a deeply moving novel."

Despite his success as a novelist, Bausch's first love has always remained the short story. "Writing them satisfies me in a way that no other activity does," he confesses. "Every stage of a story is fun to me." Over the years his work has appeared in *The Atlantic Monthly, Esquire,* and *The New Yorker,* and has also been widely anthologized. Two of the writer's stories were chosen for inclusion in *The Best American Short Stories of 1990,* and others have been featured in editions of *Prize Stories: The O. Henry Awards.* Bausch's first book of short fiction, *Spirits and Other Stories,* came out in 1987 to wide acclaim and was nominated for the PEN/Faulkner Award.

"Several of these stories rank with the best written in contemporary American fiction," said Louise Erdrich. "Bausch is a master." Walker Percy concurred: "Some of these stories are actually breathtaking in their poignancy." A second compilation, *The Fireman's Wife and Other Stories,* was published in 1990. "We are fortunate to have this impressive collection with which to explore and search for the meaning of how we live today," said *The New York Times Book Review.*

Meanwhile, Bausch continued writing novels. In *Mr. Field's Daughter* (1989) he explored the bewildering knots of emotion that bind fathers and daughters together. "Richard Bausch's fourth novel is an exceptionally mature and satisfying book, one that pays no discernible heed to prevailing literary fashion but roots itself in the solid, unpretentious, fertile ground of ordinary American middle-class life," wrote Jonathan Yardley in *The Washington Post Book World.* "Bausch has constructed a novel of relentless narrative power and psychological insight," said *The New York Times Book Review.* "Taut, compelling and entirely credible, it reveals an author of rare and penetrating gifts, working at the height of his powers." *Violence* (1992), Bausch's fifth novel, attempts to make sense of the seemingly senseless brutality built into the contemporary American landscape. "Bausch explores both the public and private manifestations of violence with persistence and sensitivity," noted *The New York Times Book Review.* "And he does so with a redeeming grace of language and detail that goes beyond mere witnessing, straight to the heart." His latest novel, *Rebel Powers* (1993), is the story of the dissolution of a family during the Vietnam war—a time when America itself was in the process of coming apart.

"Bausch's strengths are prodigious in *Rebel Powers*," said the *San Francisco Chronicle*. "This is a full, meaningful work by a mature artist about issues that plague us all." And *The Washington Post Book World* wrote: "There is in *Rebel Powers* so much to celebrate. . . . Bausch is a virtuoso of language and form whose literary grace is perfectly matched by startling intuitive powers."

Rare & Endangered Species, Bausch's most recent book, appeared in 1994. Comprising a novella and eight short stories it reveals the high hopes and suppressed panic, the good humor and last-minute improvisations with which ordinary Americans go about their not-so-ordinary lives. "*Rare & Endangered Species* demonstrates Mr. Bausch's . . . balance of soul and skill, heart and technique," said the *Washington Times*. "He has developed the emotional equivalent of perfect pitch." And the *Los Angeles Times* predicted: "This third collection by Richard Bausch will surely solidify his position as one of the best short-story writers working today."

ACKNOWLEDGMENT

Karen

CONTENTS

THE SELECTED STORIES
OF
RICHARD BAUSCH

The Man Who Knew Belle Starr

Mcrae picked up a hitcher on his way west. It was a young woman, carrying a paper bag and a leather purse, wearing jeans and a shawl—which she didn't take off, though it was more than ninety degrees out, and Mcrae had no air conditioning. He was driving an old Dodge Charger with a bad exhaust system, and one long crack in the wrap-around windshield. He pulled over for her and she got right in, put the leather purse on the seat between them, and settled herself with the paper bag on her lap between her hands. He had just crossed into Texas.

"Where you headed," he said.

She said, "What about you?"

"Nevada, maybe."

"Why maybe?"

And that fast he was answering *her* questions. "I just got out of the Air Force," he told her, though this wasn't exactly true. The Air Force had put him out with a dishonorable discharge after four years at Leavenworth for assaulting a staff sergeant. He was a bad character. He had a bad temper that had got him into a load of trouble already and he just wanted to get out west, out to the wide-open spaces. It was just to see it, really. He had the feeling people didn't require as much from a person way out where there was that kind of room. He didn't have any family now. He had five thousand dollars from his father's insurance policy, and he was going to make the money last him awhile. He said, "I'm sort of undecided about a lot of things."

"Not me," she said.

"You figured out where you were going," he said.

"You could say that."

"So where might that be."

She made a fist and then extended her thumb, and turned it over. "Under," she said; "down."

"Excuse me?"

"Does the radio work?" she asked, reaching for it.

"It's on the blink," he said.

She turned the knob anyway, then sat back and folded her arms over the paper bag.

He took a glance at her. She was skinny and long-necked,

and her hair was the color of water in a metal pail. She looked just old enough for high school.

"What's in the bag?" he said.

She sat up a little. "Nothing. Another blouse."

"Well, so what did you mean back there?"

"Back where?"

"Look," he said, "we don't have to do any talking if you don't want to."

"Then what will we do?"

"Anything you want," he said.

"What if I just want to sit here and let you drive me all the way to Nevada?"

"That's fine," he said. "That's just fine."

"Well, I won't do that. We can talk."

"Are *you* going to Nevada?" he asked.

She gave a little shrug of her shoulders. "Why not?"

"All right," he said, and for some reason he offered her his hand. She looked at it, and then smiled at him, and he put his hand back on the wheel.

IT GOT A LITTLE AWKWARD almost right away. The heat was awful, and she sat there sweating, not saying much. He never thought he was very smooth or anything, and he had been in prison: it had been a long time since he had found himself in the company of a woman. Finally she fell asleep, and for a few miles he could look at her without worrying about anything but staying on the road. He decided that she was kind of good-looking around the eyes and mouth. If she ever filled out, she might be something. He caught himself wondering what might happen, thinking of sex. A girl who traveled alone like this was probably pretty loose. Without quite realizing it, he began to daydream about her, and when he got aroused by the daydream he tried to concentrate on figuring his chances, playing his cards right, not messing up any opportunities—but being gentlemanly, too. He was not the sort of person who forced himself on young women. She slept very quietly, not breathing loudly or sighing or moving much; and then she simply sat up and folded her arms over the bag again and stared out at the road.

"God," she said, "I went out."

"You hungry?" he asked.

"No."

"What's your name?" he said. "I never got your name."

"Belle Starr," she said, and, winking at him, she made a clicking sound out of the side of her mouth.

"Belle Starr," he said.

"Don't you know who Belle Starr was?"

All he knew was that it was a familiar-sounding name. "Belle Starr."

She put her index finger to the side of his head and said, "Bang."

"Belle Starr," he said.

"Come on," she said. "Annie Oakley. Wild Bill Hickok."

"Oh," Mcrae said. "Okay."

"That's me," she said, sliding down in the seat. "Belle Starr."

"That's not your real name."

"It's the only one I go by these days."

They rode on in silence for a time.

"What's *your* name?" she said.

He told her.

"Irish?"

"I never thought about it."

"Where you from, Mcrae?"

"Washington, D.C."

"Long way from home."

"I haven't been there in years."

"Where *have* you been?"

"Prison," he said. He hadn't known he would say it, and now that he had, he kept his eyes on the road. He might as well have been posing for her; he had an image of himself as he must look from the side, and he shifted his weight a little, sucked in his belly. When he stole a glance at her he saw that she was simply gazing out at the Panhandle, one hand up like a visor to shade her eyes.

"What about you?" he said, and felt like somebody in a movie—two people with a past come together on the open road. He wondered how he could get the talk around to the subject of love.

"What *about* me?"

"Where're you from?"

"I don't want to bore you with all the facts," she said.

"I don't mind," Mcrae said. "I got nothing else to do."

"I'm from way up North."

"Okay," he said, "you want me to guess?"

"Maine," she said. "Land of Moose and Lobster."

He said, "Maine. Well, now."

"See?" she said. "The facts are just a lot of things that don't change."

"Unless you change them," Mcrae said.

She reached down and, with elaborate care, as if it were

fragile, put the paper bag on the floor. Then she leaned back and put her feet up on the dash. She was wearing low-cut tennis shoes.

"You going to sleep?" he asked.

"Just relaxing," she said.

But a moment later, when he asked if she wanted to stop and eat, she didn't answer, and he looked over to see that she was sound asleep.

HIS FATHER HAD DIED while he was at Leavenworth. The last time Mcrae saw him, he was lying on a gurney in one of the bays of D.C. General's emergency ward, a plastic tube in his mouth, an I.V. set into an ugly yellow-blue bruise on his wrist. Mcrae had come home on leave from the Air Force—which he had joined at the order of a juvenile judge—to find his father on the floor in the living room, in a pile of old newspapers and bottles, wearing his good suit, with no socks or shoes and no shirt. It looked as if he were dead. But the ambulance drivers found a pulse, and rushed him off to the hospital. Mcrae cleaned the house up a little, and then followed in the Charger. The old man had been steadily going downhill from the time Mcrae was a boy, and so this latest trouble wasn't new. In the hospital, they got the tube into his mouth and hooked him to the I.V., and then left him there on the gurney. Mcrae stood at his side, still in uniform, and when the old man opened his eyes and looked at him it was clear that he didn't know who it was. The old man blinked, stared, and then sat up, took the tube out of his mouth, and spat something terrible-looking into a small metal dish which was suspended from the complicated apparatus of the room, and which made a continual water-dropping sound like a leaking sink. He looked at Mcrae again, and then he looked at the tube. "Jesus Christ," he said.

"Hey," Mcrae said.

"What."

"It's me."

The old man put the tube back into his mouth and looked away.

"Pops," Mcrae said. He didn't feel anything.

The tube came out. "Don't look at me, boy. You got yourself into it. Getting into trouble, stealing and running around. You got yourself into it."

"I don't mind it, Pops. It's three meals and a place to sleep."

"Yeah," the old man said, and then seemed to gargle something. He spit into the little metal dish again.

"I got thirty days of leave, Pops."

"Eh?"

"I don't have to go back for a month."

"Where you going?"

"Around," Mcrae said.

The truth was that he hated the Air Force, and he was thinking of taking the Charger and driving to Canada or someplace like that, and hiding out the rest of his life—the Air Force felt like punishment, it *was* punishment, and he had already been in trouble for his quick temper and his attitude. That afternoon, he'd left his father to whatever would happen, got into the Charger, and started north. But he hadn't made it. He'd lost heart a few miles south of New York City, and he turned around and came back. The old man had been moved to a room in the alcoholic ward, but Mcrae didn't go to see him. He stayed in the house, watching television and drinking beer, and when old high school buddies came by he went around with them a little. Mostly he stayed home, though, and at the end of his leave he locked the place and drove back to Chanute, in Illinois, where he was stationed. He wasn't there two months before the staff sergeant caught him drinking beer in the dayroom of one of the training barracks, and asked for his name. Mcrae walked over to him, said, "My name is trouble," and at the word *trouble*, struck the other man in the face. He'd had a lot of the beer, and he had been sitting there in the dark, drinking the last of it, going over everything in his mind, and the staff sergeant, a baby-faced man with a spare tire of flesh around his waist and an attitude about the stripes on his sleeves, had just walked into it. Mcrae didn't even know him. Yet he stood over the sergeant where he had fallen, and then started kicking him. It took two other men to get him off the poor man, who wound up in the hospital with a broken jaw (the first punch had done it), a few cracked ribs, and multiple lacerations and bruises. The court-martial was swift. The sentence was four years at hard labor, along with the dishonorable discharge. He'd had less than a month to go on the sentence when he got the news about his father. He felt no surprise, nor, really, any grief; yet there was a little thrill of something like fear: he was in his cell, and for an instant some part of him actually wanted to remain there, inside walls, where things were certain, and there weren't any decisions to make. A week later, he learned of the money from the insurance, which would have been more than the five thousand except that his father had been a few months behind on the rent, and on other payments. Mcrae settled what he had to of those things, and kept the rest. He had started to feel like a happy man, out of Leavenworth and the Air Force, and now he was on his way to Nevada, or someplace like that—and he had picked up a girl.

HE DROVE ON UNTIL DUSK, stopping only for gas, and the girl slept right through. Just past the line into New Mexico, he pulled off the interstate and went north for a mile or so, looking for some place other than a chain restaurant to eat. She sat up straight, pushed the hair back away from her face. "Where are we?"

"New Mexico," he said. "I'm looking for a place to eat."

"I'm not hungry."

"Well," he said, "*you* might be able to go all day without anything to eat, but I got a three-meal-a-day habit to support."

She brought the paper bag up from the floor and held it in her lap.

"You got food in there?" he asked.

"No."

"You're very pretty—child-like, sort of—when you sleep."

"I didn't snore?"

"You were quiet as a mouse."

"And you think I'm pretty."

"I guess you know a thing like that. I hope I didn't offend you."

"I don't like dirty remarks," she said. "But I don't guess you meant to be dirty."

"Dirty."

"Sometimes people can say a thing like that and mean it very dirty, but I could tell you didn't."

He pulled in at a roadside diner and turned off the ignition. "Well?" he said.

She sat there with the bag on her lap. "I don't think I'll go in with you."

"You can have a cold drink or something," he said.

"You go in. I'll wait out here."

"Come on in there with me and have a cold drink," Mcrae said. "I'll buy it for you. I'll buy you dinner if you want."

"I don't want to," she said.

He got out and started for the entrance, and before he reached it he heard her door open and close, and turned to watch her come toward him, thin and waif-like in the shawl, which hid her arms and hands.

The diner was empty. There was a long, low bar, with soda fountains on the other side of it, and glass cases in which pies and cakes were set. There were booths along one wall. Everything seemed in order, except that no one was around. Mcrae and the girl stood in the doorway for a moment and waited, and finally she stepped in and took a seat in the first booth. "I guess we're supposed to seat ourselves," she said.

"This is weird," said Mcrae.

"Hey," she said, rising, "there's a jukebox." She strode over to it and leaned on it, crossing one leg behind the other at the ankle, her hair falling down to hide her face.

"Hello?" Mcrae said. "Anybody here?"

"Got any change?" asked the girl.

He gave her a quarter, and then sat at the bar. The door at the far end swung in, and a big, red-faced man entered, wearing a white cook's apron over a sweat-stained baby-blue shirt, whose sleeves he had rolled up past the meaty curve of his elbows. "Yeah?" he said.

"You open?" Mcrae asked.

"That jukebox don't work, honey," the man said.

"You open?" Mcrae said, as the girl came and sat down beside him.

"Sure, why not?"

"Place is kind of empty."

"What do you want to eat?"

"You got a menu?"

"You want a menu?"

"Sure," Mcrae said, "why not?"

"Truth is," the big man said, "I'm selling this place. I don't have menus anymore. I make hamburgers and breakfast stuff. Some french fries and cold drinks. A hot dog maybe. I'm not keeping track."

"Let's go somewhere else," the girl said.

"Yeah," said the big man, "why don't you do that."

"Look," said Mcrae, "what's the story here?"

The other man shrugged. "You came in at the end of the run, you know what I mean? I'm going out of business. Sit down and I'll make you a hamburger on the house."

Mcrae looked at the girl.

"Okay," she said, in a tone which made it clear that she would've been happier to leave.

The big man put his hands on the bar and leaned toward her. "Miss, if I were you I wouldn't look a gift horse in the mouth."

"I don't like hamburger," she said.

"You want a hot dog?" the man said. "I got a hot dog for you. Guaranteed to please."

"I'll have some french fries," she said.

The big man turned to the grill and opened the metal

drawer under it. He was very wide at the hips, and his legs were like trunks. "I get out of the Army after twenty years," he said, "and I got a little money put aside. The wife and I decide we want to get into the restaurant business. The government's going to be paying me a nice pension and we got the savings, so we sink it all in this goddamn diner. Six and a half miles from the interstate. You get the picture? The guy's selling us this diner at a great price, you know? A terrific price. For a song, I'm in the restaurant business. The wife will cook the food, and I'll wait tables, you know, until we start to make a little extra, and then we'll hire somebody—a high school kid or somebody like that. We might even open another restaurant if the going gets good enough. But of course, this is New Mexico. This is six and a half miles from the interstate. There's nothing here anymore because there's nothing up the road. You know what's up the road? Nothing." He had put the hamburger on, and a basket of frozen french fries. "Now the wife decides she's had enough of life on the border, and off she goes to Seattle to sit in the rain with her mother and here I am trying to sell a place nobody else is dumb enough to buy. You know what I mean?"

"That's rough," Mcrae said.

"You're the second customer I've had all *week,* bub."

The girl said, "I guess that cash register's empty then, huh."

"It ain't full, honey."

She got up and wandered across the room. For a while she stood gazing out the windows over the booths, her hands invisible under the woolen shawl. When she came back to sit next to Mcrae again, the hamburger and french fries were ready.

"On the house," the big man said.

And the girl brought a gun out of the shawl—a pistol that looked like a toy. "Suppose you open up that register, Mr. Poormouth," she said.

The big man looked at her, then at Mcrae, who had taken a large bite of his hamburger, and had it bulging in his cheeks.

"This thing is loaded, and I'll use it."

"Well for Christ's sake," the big man said.

Mcrae started to get off the stool. "Hold on a minute," he said to them both, his words garbled by the mouthful of food, and then everything started happening all at once. The girl aimed the pistol. There was a popping sound—a single, small pop, not much louder than the sound of a cap gun—and the big man took a step back, against the counter, into the dishes and pans there. He stared at the girl, wide-eyed, for what seemed a long time, then went down, pulling dishes with him in a tremendous shattering.

"Jesus Christ," Mcrae said, swallowing, standing back from her, raising his hands.

She put the pistol back in her jeans under the shawl, and then went around the counter and opened the cash register. "Damn," she said.

Mcrae said, low, "Jesus Christ."

And now she looked at him; it was as if she had forgotten he was there. "What're you standing there with your hands up like that?"

"God," he said, "oh, God."

"Stop it," she said. "Put your hands down."

He did so.

"Cash register's empty." She sat down on one of the stools

and gazed over at the body of the man where it had fallen. "Damn."

"Look," Mcrae said, "take my car. You—you can have my car."

She seemed puzzled. "I don't want your car. What do I want your car for?"

"You—" he said. He couldn't talk, couldn't focus clearly, or think. He looked at the man, who lay very still, and then he began to cry.

"Will you stop it?" she said, coming off the stool, reaching under the shawl and bringing out the pistol again.

"Jesus," he said. "Good Jesus."

She pointed the pistol at his forehead. "Bang," she said. "What's my name?"

"Your—name?"

"My name."

"Belle—" he managed.

"Come on," she said. "The whole thing—you remember."

"Belle—Belle Starr."

"Right." She let the gun hand drop to her side, into one of the folds of the shawl. "I like that so much better than Annie Oakley."

"Please," Mcrae said.

She took a few steps away from him and then whirled and aimed the gun. "I think we better get out of here, what do you think?"

"Take the car," he said, almost with exasperation; it frightened him to hear it in his own voice.

"I can't drive," she said simply. "Never learned."

"Jesus," he said. It went out of him like a sigh.

"God," she said, gesturing with the pistol for him to move to the door, "it's hard to believe you were ever in *prison*."

THE ROAD WENT ON INTO THE DARK, beyond the fan of the headlights; he lost track of miles, road signs, other traffic, time; trucks came by and surprised him, and other cars seemed to materialize as they started the lane change that would bring them over in front of him. He watched their tail-lights grow small in the distance, and all the while the girl sat watching him, her hands somewhere under the shawl. For a long time there was just the sound of the rushing night air at the windows, and then she moved a little, shifted her weight, bringing one leg up on the seat.

"What were you in prison for, anyway?"

Her voice startled him, and for a moment he couldn't think to answer.

"Come on," she said, "I'm getting bored with all this quiet. What were you in prison for?"

"I—beat up a guy."

"That's all?"

"Yes, that's all." He couldn't keep the irritation out of his voice.

"Tell me about it."

"It was just—I just beat up a guy. It wasn't anything."

"I didn't shoot that man for money, you know."

Mcrae said nothing.

"I shot him because he made a nasty remark to me about the hot dogs."

"I didn't hear any nasty remark."

"He shouldn't have said it or else he'd still be alive."

Mcrae held tight to the wheel.

"Don't you wish it was the Wild West?" she said.

"Wild West," he said, "yeah." He could barely speak for the dryness in his mouth and the deep ache of his own breathing.

"You know," she said, "I'm not really from Maine."

He nodded.

"I'm from Florida."

"Florida," he managed.

"Yes, only I don't have a Southern accent, so people think I'm not from there. Do you hear any trace of a Southern accent at all when I talk?"

"No," he said.

"Now you—you've got an accent. A definite Southern accent."

He was silent.

"Talk to me," she said.

"What do you want me to say?" he said. "Jesus."

"You could ask me things."

"Ask you things—"

"Ask me what my name is."

Without hesitating, Mcrae said, "What's your name?"

"You know."

"No, really," he said, trying to play along.

"It's Belle Starr."

"Belle Starr," he said.

"Nobody *but*," she said.

"Good," he said.

"And I don't care about money, either," she said. "That's not what I'm after."

"No," Mcrae said.

"What I'm after is adventure."

"Right," said Mcrae.

"Fast living."

"Fast living, right."

"A good time."

"Good," he said.

"I'm going to live a ton before I die."

"A ton, yes."

"What about you?" she said.

"Yes," he said. "Me too."

"Want to join up with me?"

"Join up," he said. "Right." He was watching the road.

She leaned toward him a little. "Do you think I'm lying about my name?"

"No."

"Good," she said.

He had begun to feel as though he might start throwing up what he'd had of the hamburger. His stomach was cramping on him, and he was dizzy. He might even be having a heart attack.

"Your eyes are big as saucers," she said.

He tried to narrow them a little. His whole body was shaking now.

"You know how old I am, Mcrae? I'm nineteen."

He nodded, glanced at her and then at the road again.

"How old are you?"

"Twenty-three."

"Do you believe people go to heaven when they die?"

"Oh, God," he said.

"Look, I'm not going to shoot you while you're driving the car. We'd crash if I did that."

"Oh," he said. "Oh, Jesus, please—look. I never saw anybody shot before—"

"Will you *stop it*?"

He put one hand to his mouth. He was soaked; he felt the sweat on his upper lip, and then he felt the dampness all through his clothes.

She said, "I don't kill everybody I meet, you know."

"No," he said. "Of course not." The absurdity of this exchange almost brought a laugh up out of him. It was astonishing that such a thing as a laugh could be anywhere in him at such a time, but here it was, rising up in his throat like some loosened part of his anatomy. He held on with his whole mind, and it was a moment before he realized that *she* was laughing.

"Actually," she said, "I haven't killed all that many people."

"How—" he began. Then he had to stop to breathe. "How many?"

"Take a guess."

"I don't have any idea," he said.

"Well," she said, "you'll just have to guess. And you'll notice that I haven't spent any time in prison."

He was quiet.

"Guess," she said.

Mcrae said, "Ten?"

"No."

He waited.

"Come on, keep guessing."

"More than ten?"

"Maybe."

"More than ten," he said.

"Well, all right. Less than ten."

"Less than ten," he said.

"Guess," she said.

"Nine."

"No."

"Eight."

"No, not eight."

"Six?"

"Not six."

"Five?"

"Five and a half people," she said. "You almost hit it right on the button."

"Five and a half people," said Mcrae.

"Right. A kid who was hitchhiking, like me; a guy at a gas station; a dog that must've got lost—I count him as the half—another guy at a gas station; a guy that took me to a motel and made an obscene gesture to me; and the guy at the diner. That makes five and a half."

"Five and a half," Mcrae said.

"You keep repeating everything I say. I wish you'd quit that."

He wiped his hand across his mouth and then feigned a cough to keep from having to speak.

"Five and a half people," she said, turning a little in the seat, putting her knees up on the dash. "Have you ever met anybody like me? Tell the truth."

"No," Mcrae said, "nobody."

"Just think about it, Mcrae. You can say you rode with Belle Starr. You can tell your grandchildren."

He was afraid to say anything to this, for fear of changing the delicate balance of the thought. Yet he knew the worst mistake would be to say nothing at all. He was beginning to feel something of the cunning that he would need to survive, even as he knew the slightest miscalculation would mean the end of him. He said, with fake wonder, "I knew Belle Starr."

She said, "Think of it."

"Something," he said.

And she sat further down in the seat. "Amazing."

HE KEPT TO FIFTY-FIVE MILES AN HOUR, and everyone else was speeding. The girl sat straight up now, nearly facing him on the seat. For long periods she had been quiet, simply watching him drive, and soon they were going to need gas. There was now less than half a tank.

"Look at these people speeding," she said. "We're the only ones obeying the speed limit. Look at them."

"Do you want me to speed up?" he asked.

"I think they ought to get tickets for speeding, that's what I think. Sometimes I wish I was a policeman."

"Look," Mcrae said, "we're going to need gas pretty soon."

"No, let's just run it until it quits. We can always hitch a ride with somebody."

"This car's got a great engine," Mcrae said. "We might have to outrun the police, and I wouldn't want to do that in any other car."

"This old thing? It's got a crack in the windshield. The radio doesn't work."

"Right. But it's a fast car. It'll outrun a police car."

She put one arm over the seat back and looked out the rear window. "You really think the police are chasing us?"

"They might be," he said.

She stared at him a moment. "No. There's no reason. No-body saw us."

"But if somebody did—this car, I mean, it'll go like crazy."

"I'm afraid of speeding, though," she said. "Besides, you know what I found out? If you run slow enough the cops go right past you. Right on past you looking for somebody who's in a hurry. No, I think it's best if we just let it run until it quits and then get out and hitch."

Mcrae thought he knew what might happen when the gas ran out: she would make him push the car to the side of the road, and then she would walk him back into the cactus and brush there, and when they were far enough from the road, she would shoot him. He knew this as if she had spelled it all out, and he began again to try for the cunning he would need. "Belle," he said. "Why don't we lay low for a few days in Albuquerque?"

"Is that an obscene gesture?" she said.

"No!" he said, almost shouted. "No! That's—it's outlaw talk. You know. Hide out from the cops—lay low. It's—it's prison talk."

"Well, I've never been in prison."

"That's all I meant."

"You want to hide out."

"Right," he said.

"You and me?"

"You—you asked if I wanted to join up with you."

"Did I?" She seemed puzzled by this.

"Yes," he said, feeling himself press it a little. "Don't you remember?"

"I guess I do."

"You did," he said.

"I don't know."

"Belle Starr had a gang," he said.

"She did."

"I could be the first member of your gang."

She sat there thinking this over. Mcrae's blood moved at the thought that she was deciding whether or not he would live. "Well," she said, "maybe."

"You've got to have a gang, Belle."

"We'll see," she said.

A moment later, she said, "How much money do you have?"

"I have enough to start a gang."

"It takes money to start a gang?"

"Well—" He was at a loss.

"How much do you have?"

He said, "A few hundred."

"Really?" she said. "That much?"

"Just enough to—just enough to get to Nevada."

"Can I have it?"

He said, "Sure." He was holding the wheel and looking out into the night.

"And we'll be a gang?"

"Right," he said.

"I like the idea. Belle Starr and her gang."

Mcrae started talking about what the gang could do, making it up as he went along, trying to sound like all the gangster movies he'd seen. He heard himself talking about things like robbery and getaway and staying out of prison, and then, as she sat there staring at him, he started talking about being at Leavenworth, what it was like. He went on about it, the hours of forced work, and the time alone; the harsh day-to-day routines, the bad food. Before he was through, feeling the necessity of deepening her sense of him as her new accomplice—and feeling strangely as though in some way he had indeed become exactly that—he was telling her everything, all the bad times he'd had: his father's alcoholism, and growing up wanting to hit something for the anger that was in him; the years of getting into trouble; the fighting and the kicking and what it had got him. He embellished it all, made it sound worse than it really was because she seemed to be going for it, and because, telling it to her, he felt oddly sorry for himself; a version of this story of pain and neglect and lonely rage was true. He had been through a lot. And as he finished, describing for her the scene at the hospital the last time he saw his father, he was almost certain that he had struck a chord in her. He thought he saw it in the rapt expression on her face.

"Anyway," he said, and smiled at her.

"Mcrae?" she said.

"Yeah?"

"Can you pull over?"

"Well," he said, his voice shaking, "why don't we wait until it runs out of gas?"

She was silent.

"We'll be that much further down the road," he said.

"I don't really want a gang," she said. "I don't like dealing with other people that much. I mean I don't think I'm a leader."

"Oh, yes," Mcrae said. "No—you're a leader. You're definitely a leader. I was in the Air Force and I know leaders and you are definitely what I'd call a leader."

"Really?"

"Absolutely. You are leadership material all the way."

"I wouldn't have thought so."

"Definitely," he said. "Definitely a leader."

"But I don't really like people around, you know."

"That's a leadership quality. Not wanting people around. It is definitely a leadership quality."

"Boy," she said, "the things you learn."

He waited. If he could only think himself through to the way out. If he could get her to trust him, get the car stopped—be there when she turned her back.

"You want to be in my gang, huh?"

"I sure do," he said.

"Well, I guess I'll have to think about it."

"I'm surprised nobody's mentioned it to you before."

"You're just saying that."

"No, really."

"Were you ever married?" she asked.

"Married?" he said, and then stammered over the answer. "Ah—uh, no."

"You ever been in a gang before?"

"A couple times, but—but they never had good leadership."

"You're giving me a line, huh."

"No," he said, "it's true. No good leadership. It was always a problem."

"I'm tired," she said, shifting toward him a little. "I'm tired of talking."

The steering wheel was hurting the insides of his hands. He held tight, looking at the coming-on of the white stripes in the road. There were no other cars now, and not a glimmer of light anywhere beyond the headlights.

"Don't you get tired of talking, sometimes?"

"I never was much of a talker," he said.

"I guess I don't mind talking as much as I mind listening," she said.

He made a sound in his throat that he hoped she took for agreement.

"That's just when I'm tired, though."

"Why don't you take a nap," he said.

She leaned back against the door and regarded him. "There's plenty of time for that later."

"SO," HE WANTED TO SAY, "you're not going to kill me— we're a gang?"

They had gone for a long time without speaking, a nerve-wrecking hour of minutes, during which the gas gauge had sunk to just above empty; and finally she had begun talking about herself, mostly in the third person. It was hard to make sense of most of it. Yet he listened as if to instructions concerning how to extricate himself. She talked about growing up in Florida, in the country, and owning a horse; she remembered when she was taught to swim by somebody she called Bill, as if Mcrae would know who that was; and then she told him how when her father ran away with her mother's sister, her mother started having men friends over all the time. "There was a lot of obscene goings-on," she said, and her voice tightened a little.

"Some people don't care what happens to their kids," said Mcrae.

"Isn't it the truth?" she said. Then she took the pistol out of the shawl. "Take this exit."

He pulled onto the ramp and up an incline to a two-lane road that went off through the desert, toward a glow that burned on the horizon. For perhaps five miles the road was straight as a plumb line, and then it curved into long, low un-dulations of sand and mesquite and cactus.

"My mother's men friends used to do whatever they wanted to me," she said. "It went on all the time. All sorts of obscene goings-on."

Mcrae said, "I'm sorry that happened to you, Belle." And for an instant he was surprised by the sincerity of his feeling: it was as if he couldn't feel sorry enough. Yet it was genuine: it all had to do with his own unhappy story. The whole world seemed very, very sad to him. "I'm really very sorry," he said.

She was quiet a moment, as if thinking about this. Then she said, "Let's pull over now. I'm tired of riding."

"It's almost out of gas," he said.

"I know, but pull it over anyway."

"You sure you want to do that?"

"See?" she said. "That's what I mean. I wouldn't like being told what I should do all the time, or asked if I was sure of what I wanted or not."

He pulled the car over and slowed to a stop. "You're right," he said, "See? Leadership. I'm just not used to somebody with leadership qualities."

She held the gun a little toward him. He was looking at the small, dark, perfect circle of the end of the barrel. "I guess we should get out, huh," she said.

"I guess so." He hadn't even heard himself.

"Do you have any relatives left anywhere?" she said.

"No."

"Your folks are both dead?"

"Right, yes."

"Which one died first?"

"I told you," he said, "didn't I? My mother. My mother died first."

"Do you feel like an orphan?"

He sighed. "Sometimes." The whole thing was slipping away from him.

"I guess I do too." She reached back and opened her door. "Let's get out now." And when he opened his door she aimed the gun at his head. "Get out slow."

"Aw, Jesus," he said. "Look, you're not going to do this, are you? I mean I thought we were friends and all."

"Just get out real slow, like I said to."

"Okay," he said, "I'm getting out." He opened his door, and the ceiling light surprised and frightened him. Some wordless part of himself understood that this was it, and all his talk had come to nothing: all the questions she had asked him, and everything he had told her—it was all completely useless. This was going to happen to him, and it wouldn't mean anything; it would just be what happened.

"Real slow," she said. "Come on."

"Why are you doing this?" he said. "You've got to tell me that before you do it."

"Will you please get out of the car now?"

He just stared at her.

"All right, I'll shoot you where you sit."

"Okay," he said, "don't shoot."

She said in an irritable voice, as though she were talking to a recalcitrant child, "You're just putting it off."

He was backing himself out, keeping his eyes on the little barrel of the gun, and he could hear something coming, seemed to notice it in the same instant that she said, "Wait."

He stood half in and half out of the car, doing as she said, and a truck came over the hill ahead of them, a tractor-trailer, all white light and roaring.

"Stay still," she said, crouching, aiming the gun at him.

The truck came fast, was only fifty yards away, and without having to decide about it, without even knowing that he would do it, Mcrae bolted into the road. He was running: there was the exhausted sound of his own breath, the truck horn blaring, coming on, louder, the thing bearing down on him, something buzzing past his head. Time slowed. His legs faltered under him, were heavy, all the nerves gone out of them. In the light of the oncoming truck, he saw his own white hands outstretched as if to grasp something in the air before him, and then the truck was past him, the blast of air from it propelling him over the side of the road and down an embankment in high, dry grass, which pricked his skin and crackled like hay.

He was alive. He lay very still. Above him was the long shape of the road, curving off in the distance, the light of the truck going on. The noise faded and was nothing. A little wind stirred. He heard the car door close. Carefully, he got to all fours, and crawled a few yards away from where he had fallen. He couldn't be sure of which direction—he only knew he couldn't stay where he was. Then he heard what he thought were her footsteps in the road, and he froze. He lay on his side, facing the embankment. When she appeared there, he almost cried out.

"Mcrae? Did I get you?" She was looking right at where he was in the dark, and he stopped breathing. "Mcrae?"

He watched her move along the edge of the embankment.

"Mcrae?" She put one hand over her eyes, and stared at a

place a few feet over from him; then she turned and went back out of sight. He heard the car door again, and again he began to crawl farther away. The ground was cold and rough, and there was a lot of sand.

He heard her put the key in the trunk, and he stood up, began to run, he was getting away, but something went wrong in his leg, something sent him sprawling, and a sound came out of him that seemed to echo, to stay on the air, as if to call her to him. He tried to be perfectly still, tried not to breathe, hearing now the small pop of the gun. He counted the reports: one, two, three. She was just standing there at the edge of the road, firing into the dark, toward where she must have thought she heard the sound. Then she was rattling the paper bag, reloading. He could hear the click of the gun. He tried to get up, and couldn't. He had sprained his ankle, had done something very bad to it. Now he was crawling wildly, blindly through the tall grass, hearing again the small report of the pistol. At last he rolled into a shallow gully, and lay there with his face down, breathing the dust, his own voice leaving him in a whimpering animal-like sound that he couldn't stop, even as he held both shaking hands over his mouth.

"Mcrae?" She sounded so close. "Hey," she said. "Mcrae?"

He didn't move. He lay there, perfectly still, trying to stop himself from crying. He was sorry for everything he had ever done. He didn't care about the money, or the car or going out west or anything. When he lifted his head to peer over the lip of the gully, and saw that she had started down the embankment with his flashlight, moving like someone with time and the patience to use it, he lost his sense of himself as Mcrae: he was just something crippled and breathing in the dark, lying flat in a little winding gully of weeds and sand. Mcrae was gone, was someone far, far away, from ages ago—a man fresh out of prison, with the whole country to wander in, and insurance money in his pocket, who had headed west with the idea that maybe his luck, at long last, had changed.

Police Dreams

About a month before Jean left him, Casey dreamed he was sitting in the old Maverick with her and the two boys, Rodney and Michael. The boys were in back, and they were being loud, and yet Casey felt alone with his wife; it was a friendly feeling, having her there next to him in the old car, the car they'd dated in. It seemed quite normal that they should all be sitting in this car which was sold two years before Michael, who is seven years old, was born. It was quite dark, quite late. The street they were on shimmered with rain. A light was blinking nearby, at an intersection, making a haze through which someone or something moved. Things shifted, and all the warm feeling was gone; Casey tried to press the gas pedal, and couldn't, and it seemed quite logical that he couldn't. And men were opening the doors of the car. They came in on both sides. It was clear that they were going to start killing; they were just going to go ahead and kill everyone.

He woke from this dream, shaking, and lay there in the dark imagining noises in the house, intruders. Finally he made himself get up and go check things out, looking in all the closets downstairs, making sure all the doors and windows were secure. For a cold minute he peered out at the moon on the lawn, crouching by the living-room window. The whole thing was absurd: he had dreamed something awful and it was making him see and hear things. He went into the kitchen and poured himself a glass of milk, drank it down, then took a couple of gulps of water. In the boys' room, he made sure their blankets were over them; he kissed each of them on the cheek, and placed his hand for a moment (big and warm, he liked to think) across each boy's shoulder blades. Then he went back into the bedroom and lay down and looked at the clock radio beyond the curving shadow of Jean's shoulder. It was five forty-five A.M., and here he was, the father of two boys, a daddy, and he wished his own father were in the house. He closed his eyes, but knew he wouldn't sleep. What he wanted to do was reach over and kiss Jean out of sleep, but she had gone to bed with a bad anxiety attack, and she always woke up depressed afterward. There was something she had to work out; she needed his understanding. So he lay there and watched the light come, trying to understand everything, and still feeling in his nerves the nightmare he'd had. After a while, Jean stirred, reached over and turned the clock radio off before the music came on. She sat up, looked at the room as if to decide about whose it was, then got out of the bed. "Casey," she said.

"I'm up," he told her.

"Don't just say 'I'm up.'"

"I am up," Casey said, "I've been up since five forty-five."

"Well, good. Get *up* up."

He had to wake the boys and supervise their preparations for school, while Jean put her makeup on and got breakfast. Everybody had to be out the door by eight o'clock. Casey was still feeling the chill of what he had dreamed, and he put his hands up to his mouth and breathed the warmth. His stomach ached a little; he thought he might be coming down with the flu.

"Guess what I just dreamed," he said. "A truly awful thing. I mean a thing so scary—"

"I don't want to hear it, Casey."

"We were all in the old Maverick," he said.

"Please. I said no—now, I mean *no*, goddammit."

"Somebody was going to destroy us. Our family."

"I'm not listening, Casey."

"All right," he said. Then he tried a smile. "How about a kiss?"

She bent down and touched his forehead with her lips.

"That's a reception-line kiss," he said. "That's the kiss you save for when they're about to close the coffin lid on me."

"God," she said, "you are positively the most morbid human being in this world."

"I was just teasing," he said.

"What about your dream that somebody is destroying us all. Were you teasing about that too?" She was bringing what she would wear out of the closet. Each morning she would lay it all out on the bed before she put anything on, and then she would stand gazing at it for a moment, as if at a version of herself.

"I wasn't teasing about the dream," he said, "I had it, all right."

"You're still lying there," she said.

"I'll get up."

"Do."

"Are you all right?"

"Casey, do you have any idea how many times a day you ask that question? Get the boys up or I will not be all right."

He went into the boys' room and nudged and tickled and kissed them awake. Their names were spelled out in wooden letters across the headboards of their beds, except that Rodney, the younger of the two, had some time ago pulled the R down from his headboard. Because of this, Casey and Michael called him Odney. "Wake up, Odney," Casey murmured, kissing the boy's ear. "Odney, Odney, Odney." Rodney looked at him and then closed his eyes. So he stepped across the cluttered space between the two beds, to Michael, who also opened his eyes and closed them.

"I saw you," Casey said.

"It's a dream," said Michael.

Casey sat down on the edge of the bed and put his hand on the boy's chest. "Another day. Another *school* day."

"I don't want to," Michael said. "Can't we stay home today?"

"Come on. Rise and shine."

Rodney pretended to snore.

"Odney's snoring," Michael said.

Casey looked over at Rodney, who at five years old still had the plump, rounded features of a baby; and for a small, blind moment he was on the verge of tears. "Time to get up," he said, and his voice left him.

"Let's stop Odney's snoring," Michael said.

Casey carried him over to Rodney's bed, and they wrestled with Rodney, who tried to burrow under his blankets. "Odney," Casey said, "where's Odney. Where did he go?"

Rodney called for his mother, laughing, and so his father let him squirm out of the bed and run, and pretended to chase him. Jean was in the kitchen, setting bowls out, and boxes of cereal. "Casey," she said, "we don't have time for this." She sang it at him as she picked Rodney up and hugged him and carried him back into his room. "Now, get ready to go, Rodney, or Mommy won't be your protector when Daddy and Michael want to tease you."

"Blackmail," Casey said, delighted, following her into the kitchen. "Unadulterated blackmail."

"Casey, really," she said.

He put his arms around her. She stood quite still and let him kiss her on the side of the face. "I'll get them going," he said. "Okay?"

"Yes," she said, "okay."

He let go of her and she turned away, seemed already to have forgotten him. He had a sense of having badly misread her. "Jean?" he said.

"Oh, Casey, will you *please* get busy."

He went in and got the boys going. He was a little short with them both. There was just enough irritation in his voice for them to notice and grow quiet. They got themselves dressed and he brushed Rodney's hair, straightened his collar, while Michael made the beds. They all walked into the kitchen and sat at their places without speaking. Jean had poured cereal and milk, and made toast. She sat eating her cereal and reading the back of the cereal box.

"All ready," Casey said.

She nodded at him. "I called Dana and told her I'd probably be late."

"You're not going to be late."

"I don't want to have to worry about it. They're putting that tarry stuff down on the roads today, remember? I'm going to miss it. I'm going to go around the long way."

"Okay. But it's not us making you late."

"I didn't say it was, Casey."

"I don't want toast," Rodney said.

"Eat your toast," said Jean.

"I don't like it."

"Last week you loved toast."

"Nu-*uh*."

"Eat the toast, Rodney, or I'll spank you."

Michael said, "Really, Mom. He doesn't like toast."

"Eat the toast," Casey said. "Both of you. And Michael, you mind your own business."

Then they were all quiet. Outside, an already gray sky seemed to grow darker. The light above the kitchen table looked meager; it might even have flickered, and for a bad minute Casey felt the nightmare along his spine, as if the whole morning were something presented to him in the help-lessness of sleep.

HE USED TO THINK that one day he would look back on these years as the happiest time, frantic as things were: he and Jean would wonder how they'd got through it; Michael and Rodney, grown up, with children of their own, might listen to the stories and laugh. How each day of the week began with a kind of frantic rush to get everyone out the door on time. How even with two incomes there was never enough money. How time and the space in which to put things was so precious and how each weekend was like a sort of collapse, spent sleeping or watching too much television. And how, when there *was* a little time to relax, they felt in some ways just as frantic about *that,* since it would so soon be gone. Jean was working full time as a dental assistant, cleaning people's teeth and telling them what they already knew, that failure to brush and floss meant gum disease; it amazed her that so many people seemed to think no real effort or care was needed. The whole world looked lazy, negligent, to her. And then she would come home to all the things she lacked energy for. Casey, who spent his day in the offices of the Point Royal Ballet company, worrying about grants, donations, ticket sales, and promotions, would do the cooking. It was what relaxed him. Even on those days when he had to work into the evening hours—nights when the company was performing or when there was a special promotion—he liked to cook something when he got home. When Michael was a baby, Jean would sometimes get a baby-sitter for him and take the train into town on the night of a performance. Casey would meet her at the station, which was only a block away from the Hall. They would have dinner together and then they would go to the ballet.

Once, after a performance, as they were leaving the Hall, Jean turned to him and said "You know something? You know where we are? We're where they all end up—you know, the lovers in the movies. When everything works out and they get together at the end—they're headed to where we are now."

"The ballet?" he said.

"No, no, no, no, no. Married. And having babies. That. Trying to keep everything together and make ends meet, and going to the ballet and having a baby-sitter. Get it? This is where they all want to go in those movies."

He took in a deep breath of air. "We're at happily ever after, is what you're saying."

She laughed. "Casey, if only everyone was as happy as you are. I think I was complaining."

"We're smack-dab in the middle of happily ever after," Casey said, and she laughed again. They walked on, satisfied. There was snow in the street, and she put her arm in his, tucked her chin under her scarf.

"Dear, good old Casey," she said. "We don't have to go to work in the morning, and we have a little baby at home, and we're going to go there now and make love—what more could anyone ask for."

A moment later, Casey said, "Happy?"

She stopped. "Don't ask me that all the time. Can't you tell if I'm happy or not?"

"I like to hear you say you are," said Casey, "that's all."

"Well, I *are*. Now, walk." She pulled him, laughing, along the slippery sidewalk.

SOMETIMES, NOW THAT SHE'S GONE, he thinks of that night, and wonders what could ever have been going on in her mind. He wonders how she remembers that night, if she thinks about it at all. It's hard to believe the marriage is over, because nothing has been settled or established; something got under his wife's skin, something changed for her, and she had to get off on her own to figure it all out.

He had other dreams before she left, and their similarity to the first one seemed almost occult to him. In one, he and Jean and the boys were walking along a quiet, tree-shaded road; the shade grew darker, there was another intersection. Somehow they had entered a congested city street. Tenements marched up a hill to the same misty nimbus of light. Casey recognized it, and the shift took place; a disturbance, the sudden pathology of the city—gunshots, shouts. A shadow-figure arrived in a rusted-out truck and offered them a ride. The engine raced, and Casey tried to shield his family with his body. There was just the engine at his back, and then a voice whispered "Which of you wants it first?"

"A horrible dream," he said to Jean. "It keeps coming at me in different guises."

"We can't both be losing our minds," Jean said. She couldn't sleep nights. She would gladly take his nightmares if she could just sleep.

ON THE MORNING OF THE DAY SHE LEFT, he woke to find her sitting at her dressing table, staring at herself. "Honey?" he said.

"Go back to sleep," she said. "I woke the boys. It's early."

He watched her for a moment. She wasn't doing anything. She simply stared. It was as if she saw something in the mirror. "Jean," he said, and she looked at him exactly the same way she had been looking at the mirror. He said, "Why don't we go to the performance tonight?"

"I'm too tired by that time of the day," she said. Then she looked down and muttered, "I'm too tired right now."

The boys were playing in their room. In the next few minutes their play grew louder, and then they were fighting. Michael screamed; Rodney had hit him over the head with a toy fire engine. It was a metal toy, and Michael sat bleeding in the middle of the bedroom floor. Both boys were crying. Casey made Michael stand, and located the cut on his scalp. Jean had come with napkins and the hydrogen peroxide. She was very pale, all the color gone from her lips. "I'll do it," she said when Casey tried to help. "Get Rodney out of here."

He took Rodney by the hand and walked him into the living room. Rodney still held the toy fire engine, and was still crying. Casey bent down and took the toy, then moved to the sofa and sat down so that his son was facing him, standing between his knees. "Rodney," he said, "listen to me, son." The boy sniffled, and tears ran down his face. "Do you know you could have really hurt him—you could have really hurt your brother?"

"Well, he wouldn't leave me alone."

The fact that the child was unrepentant, even after having looked at his brother's blood, made Casey a little sick to his stomach. "That makes no difference," he said.

Jean came through from the hallway, carrying a bloody napkin. "Is it bad?" he said to her as she went into the kitchen. When she came back, she had a roll of paper towels. "He threw up, for Christ's sake. No, it's not bad. It's just a nick. But there's a lot of blood." She reached down and yanked Rodney away from his father. "Do you know what you did, young man? Do you? Do you?" She shook him. "Well, do you?"

"Hey," Casey said, "take it easy, honey." "Agh," she said, letting go of Rodney, "I can't stand it anymore."

Casey followed her into the bedroom, where she sat at the dressing table and began furiously to brush her hair.

"Jean," he said, "I wish we could talk."

"Oh, Jesus, Casey." She started to cry. "It's not even eight o'clock and we've already had this. It's too early for everything. I get to work and I'm exhausted. I don't even think I can stand it." She put the brush down and looked at herself, crying. "Look at me, would you? I look like death." He put his hands on her shoulders, and then Rodney was in the doorway.

"Mommy," Rodney whined.

Jean closed her eyes and shrieked, "Get out of here!"

Casey took the boy into his room. Michael was sitting on his bed, holding a napkin to his head. There was a little pool of sickness on the floor at his feet. Casey got paper towels and cleaned it up. Michael looked at him with an expression of pain, of injured dignity. Rodney sat next to Michael and folded his small hands in his lap. Both boys were quiet, and it went through Casey's mind that he could teach them something in this moment. But all he could think to say was "No more fighting."

DANA IS THE WIFE OF the dentist Jean has worked for since before she met Casey. The two women became friends while

Dana was the dentist's receptionist. The dentist and his wife live in a large house on twenty acres not far from the city. There's an indoor pool, and there are tennis courts; fireplaces in the bedrooms. There's plenty of space for Jean, who moved in on a Friday afternoon, almost a month ago now. That day she just packed a suitcase; she was simply going to spend a weekend at Dana's, to rest. It was just going to be a little relaxation, a little time away. Just the two days. But then Sunday afternoon she phoned to say she would be staying on through the week.

"You're kidding me," Casey said.

And she began to cry.

"Jean," he said, "for God's sake."

"I'm sorry," she said, crying, "I just need some time."

"Time," he said. "Jean. *Jean.*"

She breathed once, and when she spoke again there was resolution in her voice, a definiteness that made his heart hurt. "I'll be over to pick up a few things tomorrow afternoon."

"Look," he said, "what is this? What about us? What about the boys?"

"I don't think you should let them see me tomorrow. This is hard enough for them."

"*What* is, Jean."

She said nothing. He thought she might've hung up.

"Jean," he said. "Good Christ. Jean."

"Please don't do this," she said.

Casey shouted into the phone. "*You're* saying that to *me!*"

"I'm sorry," she said, and hung up.

He dialed Dana's number, and Dana answered.

"I want to speak to Jean, please."

"I'm sorry, Casey—she doesn't want to talk now."

"Would you—" he began.

"I'll ask her. I'm sorry, Casey."

"Ask her to please come to the phone."

There was a shuffling sound, and he knew Dana was holding her hand over the receiver. Then there was another shuffling, and Dana spoke to him. "I hate to be in the middle of this, Casey, but she doesn't want to talk now."

"Will you please ask her what I did."

"I can't do that. Really. Please, now."

"Just tell her I want—goddammit—I want to know what I did."

There was yet another shuffling sound, only this time Casey could hear Dana's voice, sisterly and exasperated and pleading.

"Dana," he said.

Silence.

"Dana."

And Dana's voice came back, very distraught, almost frightened. "Casey, I've never hung up on anyone in my life. I have a real fear of ever doing anything like that to anyone, but if you cuss at me again I will. I'll hang up on you. Jean isn't going to talk to anyone on the phone tonight. Really, she's not, and I don't see why I have to take the blame for it."

"Dana," he said. "I'm sorry. Tell her I'll be here tomorrow—with her children. Tell her that."

"I'll tell her."

"Goodbye, Dana." He put the receiver down. In the boys' room it was quiet, and he wondered how much they had heard, and—if they had heard enough—how much they had understood.

There was dinner to make, but he was practiced at it, so it

offered no difficulty except that he prepared it in the knowledge that his wife was having some sort of nervous breakdown, and was unreachable in a way that made him angry as much as it frightened him. The boys didn't eat the fish he fried, or the potatoes he baked. They had been sneaking cookies all day while he watched football. He couldn't eat either, and so he didn't scold them for their lack of appetite and only reprimanded them mildly for their pilferage.

Shortly after the dinner dishes were done, Michael began to cry. He said he had seen something on TV that made him sad, but he had been watching *The Dukes of Hazzard*.

"My little tenderhearted man," Casey said, putting his arms around the boy.

"Is Mommy at Dana's?" Rodney asked.

"Mommy had to go do something," Casey said.

He put them to bed. He wondered as he tucked them in if he should tell them now that their mother wouldn't be there in the morning. It seemed too much to tell a child before sleep. He stood in their doorway, imagining the shadow he made with the light behind him in the hall, and told them good night. Then he went into the living room and sat staring at the shifting figures on the television screen. Apparently, *The Dukes of Hazzard* was over; he could tell by the music that this was a serious show. A man with a gun chased another man with another gun. It was hard to tell which one was the hero, and Casey began to concentrate. It turned out that both men were gangsters, and Jean, who used to say that she only put TV on sometimes for the voices, the company at night, had just told him that she was not coming home. He turned the gangsters off in mid-chase and stood for a moment, breathing fast. The boys were whispering and talking in the other room.

"Go to sleep in there," he said, keeping his voice steady. "Don't make me have to come in there." He listened. In a little while, he knew, they would begin it all again; they would keep it up until they got sleepy. He turned the television back on, so they wouldn't have to worry that he might hear them, and then he lay back on the sofa, miserable, certain that he would be awake all night. But some time toward the middle of the late movie, he fell asleep and had another dream. It was, really, the same dream: he was with Jean and the kids in a building, and they were looking for a way out; one of the boys opened a door on empty space, and Casey, turning, understood that this place was hundreds of feet above the street; the wind blew at the opening like the wind at the open hatch of an airliner, and someone was approaching from behind them. He woke up, sweating, cold, disoriented, and saw that the TV was off. With a tremendous settling into him of relief, he thought Jean had changed her mind and come home, had turned the TV off and left him there to sleep. But the bedroom was empty. "Jean," he said into the dark, "Honey?" There wasn't anyone there. He turned the light on.

"Daddy, you fell asleep watching television," Michael said from his room.

"Oh," Casey said. "Thanks, son. Can't you sleep?"

"Yeah."

"Well—goodnight, then."

"Night."

SO JEAN IS GONE. Casey keeps the house, and the boys. He's told them their mother is away because these things happen; he's told them she needs a little time to herself. He hears Jean's explanations to him in everything he says, and there doesn't seem to be anything else to say. It's as if they were all waiting for her to get better, as if this trouble were something physiological, an illness that deprives them of her as she used to be. Casey talks to her on the phone now and then, and it's always, oddly, as if they had never known anything funny or embarrassing about each other, and yet were both, now, funny and embarrassed. They talk about the boys; they laugh too quickly and they stumble over normal exchanges, like *hello* and *how are you* and *what have you been up to.* Jean has been working longer hours, making overtime from Dana's husband. Since Dana's husband's office is right downstairs, she can go for days without leaving the house if she wants to. She's feeling rested now. The overtime keeps her from thinking too much. Two or three times a week she goes over to the boys' school and spends some time with them; she's been a room mother since Michael started there two years ago, and she still does her part whenever there's something for her to do. She told Casey over the phone that Rodney's teacher seems to have no inkling that anything has changed at home.

Casey said, "What *has* changed at home, Jean?"

"Don't be ridiculous," she said.

The boys seem, in fact, to be taking everything in stride, although Casey thinks there's a reticence about them now; he knows they're keeping their feelings mostly to themselves. Once in a while Rodney asks, quite shyly, when Mommy's coming home. Michael shushes him. Michael is being very grown up and understanding. It's as if he were five years older than he is. At night, he reads to Rodney from his Choose-

Your-Own-Adventure books. Casey sits in the living room and hears this. And when he has to work late, has to leave them with a baby-sitter, he imagines the baby-sitter hearing it, and feels soothed somehow—almost, somehow, consoled, as if simply to imagine such a scene were to bathe in its warmth: a slightly older boy reading to his brother, the two of them propped on the older brother's bed.

This is what he imagines tonight, the night of the last performance of *Swan Lake,* as he stands in the balcony and watches the Hall fill up. The Hall is sold out. Casey gazes at the crowd and it crosses his mind that all these people are carrying their own scenes, things that have nothing to do with ballet, or polite chatter, or finding a numbered seat. The fact that they all move as quietly and cordially to their places as they do seems miraculous to him. They are all in one situation or another, he thinks, and at that instant he catches sight of Jean; she's standing in the center aisle below him. Dana is with her. Jean is up on her toes, looking across to the other side of the Hall, where Casey usually sits. She turns slowly, scanning the crowd. It strikes Casey that he knows what her situation is. The crowd of others surges around her. And now Dana, also looking for him, finds him, touches Jean's shoulder and actually points at him. He feels strangely inanimate, and he steps back a little, looks away from them. A moment later, it occurs to him that this is too obviously a snub, so he steps forward again and sees that Dana is alone down there, that Jean is already lost somewhere else in the crowd. Dana is gesturing for him to remain where he is. The orchestra members begin wandering out into the pit and tuning up; there's a scattering of applause. Casey finds a seat near the railing and sits with his hands folded in his lap, waiting.

When this section of the balcony begins to fill up, he rises, looks for Dana again, and can't find her. Someone edges past him along the railing, and he moves to the side aisle, against the wall. He sees Jean come in, and watches her come around to where he is.

"I was hoping you'd be here tonight," she says, smiling. She touches his forearm, then leans up and gives him a dry little kiss on the mouth. "I wanted to see you."

"You can see me anytime," he says. He can't help the contentiousness in his voice.

"Casey," she says, "I know this is not the place—it's just that—well, Dana and I were coming to the performance, you know, and I started thinking how unfair I've been to you, and—and it just doesn't seem right."

Casey stands there looking at her.

"Can we talk a little," she says, "outside?"

He follows her up to the exit and out along the corridor to a little alcove leading into the rest rooms. There's a red velvet armchair, which she sits in, then pats her knees exactly as if she expected him to settle into her lap. But she's only smoothing her skirt over her knees, stalling. Casey pulls another chair over and then stands behind it, feeling a dizzy, unfamiliar sense of suffocation. He thinks of swallowing air, pulls his tie loose and breathes.

"Well," she says.

"The performance is going to start any minute," he says.

"I know," she says. "Casey—" She clears her throat, holding the backs of her fingers over her lips. It is a completely uncharacteristic gesture, and he wonders if she might have picked it up from Dana. "Well," she says, "I think we have to come to some sort of agreement about Michael and Rodney.

I mean seeing them in school—" She sits back, not looking at him. "You know, and talking on the phone and stuff—I mean that's no good. I mean none of this is any good. Dana and I have been talking about this quite a lot, Casey. And there's no reason, you know, that just because you and I aren't together anymore—that's no reason the kids should have to go without their mother."

"Jean," he says, "what—what—" He sits down. He wants to take her hand.

She says, "I think I ought to have them awhile. A week or two. Dana and I have discussed it, and she's amenable to the idea. There's plenty of room and everything, and pretty soon I'll be—I'll be getting a place." She moves the tip of one finger along the soft surface of the chair arm, then seems to have to fight off tears.

Casey reaches over and takes her hand. "Honey," he says.

She pulls her hand away, quite gently, but with the firmness of someone for whom this affection is embarrassing. "Did you hear me, Casey. I'm getting a place of my own. We have to decide about the kids."

Casey stares at her, watches as she opens her purse and takes out a handkerchief to wipe her eyes. It comes to him very gradually that the orchestra has commenced to play. She seems to notice it too, now. She puts the handkerchief back in her purse and snaps it shut, then seems to gather herself.

"Jean," he says, "for God's sweet sake."

"Oh, come on," she says, her eyes swimming, "you knew this was coming. How could you not know this was coming?"

"I don't believe this," he says. "You come here to tell me this. At my goddamn *job*." His voice has risen almost to a shout.

"Casey," she says.

"Okay," he says, rising. "I know you." It makes no sense. He tries to find something to say to her; he wants to say it all out in an orderly way that will show her. But he stammers. "You're not having a nervous breakdown," he hears himself tell her, and then he repeats it almost as if he were trying to reassure her. "This is really it, then," he goes on. "You're not coming back."

She stands. There's something incredulous in the way she looks at him. She steps away from him, gives him a regretful look.

"Jean, we didn't even have an argument," he says. "I mean, what is this about?"

"Casey, I was so unhappy all the time. Don't you remember anything? Don't you see how it was? And I thought it was because I wasn't a good mother. I didn't even like the sound of their voices. But it was just unhappiness. I see them at school now and I love it. It's not a chore now. I work like a dog all day and I'm not tired. Don't you see? I feel good all the time now and I don't even mind as much when I'm tired or worried."

"Then—" he begins.

"Try to understand, Casey. It was ruining me for everyone in that house. But it's okay now. I'm out of it and it's okay. I'm not dying anymore in those rooms and everything on my nerves and you around every corner—" She stops.

He can't say anything. He's left with the weight of himself, standing there before her. "You know what you sound like," he says. "You sound ridiculous, that's what you sound like." And the ineptness of what he has just said, the stupid, helpless rage of it, produces in him a tottering moment of wanting to put his hands around her neck. The idea comes to him so clearly that his throat constricts, and a fan of heat opens across the back of his head. He holds on to the chair back and seems to hear her say that she'll be in touch, through a lawyer if that will make it easier, about arrangements concerning the children.

He knows it's not cruelty that brought her here to tell him a thing like this, it's cowardice. "I wish there was some other way," she tells him, then turns and walks along the corridor to the stairs and down. He imagines the look she'll give Dana when she gets to her seat; she'll be someone relieved of a situation, glad something's over with.

Back in the balcony, in the dark, he watches the figures leap and stutter and whirl on the stage. And when the performance ends he watches the Hall empty out. The musicians pack their music and instruments; the stage crew dismantles the set. When he finally rises, it's past midnight. Everyone's gone. He makes his way home, and, arriving, doesn't remember driving there. The baby-sitter, a high school girl from up the street, is asleep on the sofa in the living room. He's much later than he said he would be. She hasn't heard him come in, and so he has to try to wake her without frightening her. He has this thought clear in his mind as he watches his hand roughly grasp her shoulder, and hears himself say, loud, "Get up!"

The girl opens her eyes and looks blankly at him, and then she screams. He would never have believed this of himself. She is sitting up now, still not quite awake, her hands flying up to her face. "I didn't mean to scare you," he says, but it's obvious that he did mean to scare her, and while she struggles to get her shoes on, her hands shaking, he counts out the money to pay her. He gives her an extra five dollars, and she thanks him for it in a tone that lets him know it mitigates nothing. When he moves to the door with her, she tells him she'll walk home; it's only up the block. Her every movement expresses her fear of him now. She lets herself out, and Casey stands in his doorway under the porch light and calls after her that he is so very sorry, he hopes she'll forgive him. She goes quickly along the street and is out of sight. Casey stands there and looks at the place where she disappeared. Perhaps a minute goes by. Then he closes the door and walks back through the house, to the boys' room.

Rodney is in Michael's bed with Michael, the two of them sprawled there, arms and legs tangled, blankets knotted and wrapped, the sheet pulled from a corner of the mattress. It's as if this had all been dropped from a great, windy height. Casey kisses his sons, and then gets into Rodney's bed. "Odney," he whispers. He looks over at the shadowy figures in the other bed. The light is still on in the hall, and in the living room. He thinks of turning the lights off, then dreams he does. He walks through the rooms, locking windows and closing doors. In the dream he's blind, can't open his eyes wide enough, can't get any light. He hears sounds. There's an intruder in the house. There are many intruders. He's in the darkest corner, and he can hear them moving toward him. He turns, still trying to get his eyes wide enough to see, only now something has changed: he knows he's dreaming. It comes to him with a rush of power that he's dreaming, and can do anything now, anything he wants to do. He luxuriates in this as he tries to hold on to it, feels how precarious it must be. He takes one step, and then another. He's in control now. He's as quiet as the sound after death. He knows he can begin, and so he begins. He glides through the house. He tracks the intruders down. He is relentless. He destroys them, one by one. He wins. He establishes order.

What Feels Like the World

Very early in the morning, too early, he hears her trying to jump rope out on the sidewalk below his bedroom window. He wakes to the sound of her shoes on the concrete, her breathless counting as she jumps—never more than three times in succession—and fails again to find the right rhythm, the proper spring in her legs to achieve the thing, to be a girl jumping rope. He gets up and moves to the window and, parting the curtain only slightly, peers out at her. For some reason he feels he must be stealthy, must not let her see him gazing at her from this window. He thinks of the heartless way children tease the imperfect among them, and then he closes the curtain.

She is his only granddaughter, the unfortunate inheritor of his big-boned genes, his tendency toward bulk, and she is on a self-induced program of exercise and dieting, to lose weight. This is in preparation for the last meeting of the PTA, during which children from the fifth and sixth grades will put on a gymnastics demonstration. There will be a vaulting horse and a mini-trampoline, and everyone is to participate. She wants to be able to do at least as well as the other children in her class, and so she has been trying exercises to improve her co-ordination and lose the weight that keeps her rooted to the ground. For the past two weeks she has been eating only one meal a day, usually lunch, since that's the meal she eats at school, and swallowing cans of juice at other mealtimes. He's afraid of anorexia but trusts her calm determination to get ready for the event. There seems no desperation, none of the classic symptoms of the disease. Indeed, this project she's set for herself seems quite sane: to lose ten pounds, and to be able to get over the vaulting horse—in fact, she hopes that she'll be able to do a handstand on it and, curling her head and shoulders, flip over to stand upright on the other side. This, she has told him, is the outside hope. And in two weeks of very grown-up discipline and single-minded effort, that hope has mostly disappeared; she's still the only child in the fifth grade who has not even been able to propel herself over the horse, and this is the day of the event. She will have one last chance to practice at school today, and so she's up this early, out on the lawn, straining, pushing herself.

He dresses quickly and heads downstairs. The ritual in the

mornings is simplified by the fact that neither of them is eating breakfast. He makes the orange juice, puts vitamins on a saucer for them both. When he glances out the living-room window, he sees that she is now doing somersaults in the dewy grass. She does three of them while he watches, and he isn't stealthy this time but stands in the window with what he hopes is an approving, unworried look on his face. After each somersault she pulls her sweat shirt down, takes a deep breath, and begins again, the arms coming down slowly, the head ducking slowly under; it's as if she falls on her back, sits up, and then stands up. Her cheeks are ruddy with effort. The moistness of the grass is on the sweat suit, and in the ends of her hair. It will rain this morning—there's thunder beyond the trees at the end of the street. He taps on the window, gestures, smiling, for her to come in. She waves at him, indicates that she wants him to watch her, so he watches her. He applauds when she's finished—three hard, slow tumbles. She claps her hands together as if to remove dust from them and comes trotting to the door. As she moves by him, he tells her she's asking for a bad cold, letting herself get wet so early in the morning. It's his place to nag. Her glance at him acknowledges this.

"I can't get the rest of me to follow my head," she says about the somersaults.

They go into the kitchen, and she sits down, pops a vitamin into her mouth, and takes a swallow of the orange juice. "I guess I'm not going to make it over that vaulting horse after all," she says suddenly.

"Sure you will."

"I don't care." She seems to pout. This is the first sign of true discouragement she's shown.

He's been waiting for it. "Brenda—honey, sometimes people aren't good at these things. I mean, I was never any good at it."

"I bet you were," she says. "I bet you're just saying that to make me feel better."

"No," he says, "really."

He's been keeping to the diet with her, though there have been times during the day when he's cheated. He no longer has a job, and the days are long; he's hungry all the time. He pretends to her that he's still going on to work in the mornings after he walks her to school, because he wants to keep her sense of the daily balance of things, of a predictable and orderly routine, intact. He believes this is the best way to deal with grief—simply to go on with things, to keep them as much as possible as they have always been. Being out of work doesn't worry him, really: he has enough money in savings to last awhile. At sixty-one, he's almost eligible for Social Security, and he gets monthly checks from the girl's father, who lives with another woman, and other children, in Oregon. The father has been very good about keeping up the payments, though he never visits or calls. Probably he thinks the money buys him the privilege of remaining aloof, now that Brenda's mother is gone. Brenda's mother used to say he was the type of man who learned early that there was nothing of substance anywhere in his soul, and spent the rest of his life trying to hide this fact from himself. No one was more upright, she would say, no one more honorable, and God help you if you ever had to live with him. Brenda's father was the subject of bitter sarcasm and scorn. And yet, perhaps not so surprisingly, Brenda's mother would call him in those months just after the divorce, when Brenda was still only a toddler, and she would try to get the baby to say things to him over the phone. And she would sit there with Brenda on her lap and cry after she had hung up.

"I had a doughnut yesterday at school," Brenda says now.

"That's lunch. You're supposed to eat lunch."

"I had spaghetti, too. And three pieces of garlic bread. And pie. And a big salad."

"What's one doughnut?"

"Well, and I didn't eat anything the rest of the day."

"I know," her grandfather says. "See?"

They sit quiet for a little while. Sometimes they're shy with each other—more so lately. They're used to the absence of her mother by now—it's been almost a year—but they still find themselves missing a beat now and then, like a heart with a valve almost closed. She swallows the last of her juice and then gets up and moves to the living room, to stand gazing out at the yard. Big drops have begun to fall. It's a storm, with rising wind and, now, very loud thunder. Lightning branches across the sky, and the trees in the yard disappear in sheets of rain. He has come to her side, and he pretends an interest in the details of the weather, remarking on the heaviness of the rain, the strength of the wind. "Some storm," he says finally. "I'm glad we're not out in it." He wishes he could tell what she's thinking, where the pain is; he wishes he could be certain of the harmlessness of his every word. "Honey," he ventures, "we could play hooky today. If you want to."

"Don't you think I can do it?" she says.

"I know you can."

She stares at him a moment and then looks away, out at the storm.

"It's terrible out there, isn't it?" he says. "Look at that lightning."

"You don't think I can do it," she says.

"No. I know you can. Really."

"Well, I probably can't."

"Even if you can't. Lots of people—lots of people never do anything like that."

"I'm the only one who can't that *I* know."

"Well, there's lots of people. The whole thing is silly, Brenda. A year from now it won't mean anything at all—you'll see."

She says nothing.

"Is there some pressure at school to do it?"

"No." Her tone is simple, matter-of-fact, and she looks directly at him.

"You're sure."

She's sure. And of course, he realizes, there *is* pressure; there's the pressure of being one among other children, and being the only one among them who can't do a thing.

"Honey," he says, lamely, "it's not that important."

When she looks at him this time, he sees something scarily unchildlike in her expression, some perplexity that she seems to pull down into herself. "It is too important," she says.

HE DRIVES HER TO SCHOOL. The rain is still being blown along the street and above the low roofs of the houses. By the time they arrive, no more than five minutes from the house, it has begun to let up.

"If it's completely stopped after school," she says, "can we walk home?"

"Of course," he says. "Why wouldn't we?"

She gives him a quick wet kiss on the cheek. "Bye, Pops."

He knows she doesn't like it when he waits for her to get inside, and still he hesitates. There's always the apprehension that he'll look away or drive off just as she thinks of something she needs from him, or that she'll wave to him and he won't see her. So he sits here with the car engine idling, and she walks quickly up the sidewalk and into the building. In the few seconds before the door swings shut, she turns and gives him a wave, and he waves back. The door is closed now. Slowly he lets the car glide forward, still watching the door. Then he's down the driveway, and he heads back to the house.

IT'S HARD TO DECIDE what to do with his time. Mostly he stays in the house, watches television, reads the newspapers. There are household tasks, but he can't do anything she might notice, since he's supposed to be at work during these hours. Sometimes, just to please himself, he drives over to the bank and visits with his old co-workers, though there doesn't seem to be much to talk about anymore and he senses that he makes them all uneasy. Today he lies down on the sofa in the living room and rests awhile. At the windows the sun begins to show, and he thinks of driving into town, perhaps stopping somewhere to eat a light breakfast. He accuses himself with the thought and then gets up and turns on the television. There isn't anything of interest to watch, but he watches anyway. The sun is bright now out on the lawn, and the wind is the same, gusting and shaking the window frames. On television he sees feasts of incredible sumptuousness, almost nauseating in the impossible brightness and succulence of the food: advertisements from cheese companies, dairy associations, the makers of cookies and pizza, the sellers of seafood and steaks. He's angry with himself for wanting to cheat on the diet. He thinks of Brenda at school, thinks of crowds of children, and it comes to him more painfully than ever that he can't protect her. Not any more than he could ever protect her mother.

He goes outside and walks up the drying sidewalk to the end of the block. The sun has already dried most of the morning's rain, and the wind is warm. In the sky are great stormy Matterhorns of cumulus and wide patches of the deepest blue. It's a beautiful day, and he decides to walk over to the school. Nothing in him voices this decision; he simply begins to walk. He knows without having to think about it that he can't allow her to see him, yet he feels compelled to take the risk that she might; he feels a helpless wish to watch over her, and, beyond this, he entertains the vague notion that by seeing her in her world he might be better able to be what she needs in his.

So he walks the four blocks to the school and stands just beyond the playground, in a group of shading maples that whisper and sigh in the wind. The playground is empty. A bell rings somewhere in the building, but no one comes out. It's not even eleven o'clock in the morning. He's too late for morning recess and too early for the afternoon one. He feels as though she watches him make his way back down the street.

HIS NEIGHBOR, MRS. EBERHARD, comes over for lunch. It's a thing they planned, and he's forgotten about it. She knocks on the door, and when he opens it she smiles and says, "I knew you'd forget." She's on a diet too, and is carrying what they'll eat: two apples, some celery and carrots. It's all in a clear plastic bag, and she holds it toward him in the palms of her hands as though it were piping hot from an oven. Jane Eberhard is relatively new in the neighborhood. When Brenda's mother died, Jane offered to cook meals and regulate things, and for a while she was like another member of the family. She's moved into their lives now, and sometimes they all forget the circumstances under which the friendship began. She's a solid, large-hipped woman of fifty-eight, with clear, young blue eyes and gray hair. The thing she's good at is sympathy; there's something oddly unspecific about it, as if it were a beam she simply radiates.

"You look so worried," she says now, "I think you should be proud of her."

They're sitting in the living room, with the plastic bag on the coffee table before them. She's eating a stick of celery.

"I've never seen a child that age put such demands on herself," she says.

"I don't know what it's going to do to her if she doesn't make it over the damn thing," he says.

"It'll disappoint her. But she'll get over it."

"I don't guess you can make it tonight."

"Can't," she says. "Really. I promised my mother I'd take her to the ocean this weekend. I have to go pick her up tonight."

"I walked over to the school a little while ago."

"Are you sure you're not putting more into this than she is?"

"She was up at dawn this morning, Jane. Didn't you see her?"

Mrs. Eberhard nods. "I saw her."

"Well?" he says.

She pats his wrist. "I'm sure it won't matter a month from now."

"No," he says, "that's not true. I mean, I wish I could believe you. But I've never seen a kid work so hard."

"Maybe she'll make it."

"Yes," he says. "Maybe."

Mrs. Eberhard sits considering for a moment, tapping the stick of celery against her lower lip. "You think it's tied to the accident in some way, don't you?"

"I don't know," he says, standing, moving across the room. "I can't get through somehow. It's been all this time and I still don't know. She keeps it all to herself—all of it. All I can do is try to be there when she wants me to be there. I don't know—I don't even know what to say to her."

"You're doing all you can do, then."

"Her mother and I . . ." he begins. "She—we never got along that well."

"You can't worry about that now."

Mrs. Eberhard's advice is always the kind of practical good advice that's impossible to follow.

He comes back to the sofa and tries to eat one of the apples, but his appetite is gone. This seems ironic to him. "I'm not hungry now," he says.

"Sometimes worry is the best thing for a diet."

"I've always worried. It never did me any good, but I worried."

"I'll tell you," Mrs. Eberhard says. "It's a terrific misfortune to have to be raised by a human being."

He doesn't feel like listening to this sort of thing, so he asks

her about her husband, who is with the government in some
capacity that requires him to be both secretive and mobile.
He's always off to one country or another, and this week he's
in India. It's strange to think of someone traveling as much as
he does without getting hurt or killed. Mrs. Eberhard says
she's so used to his being gone all the time that next year,
when he retires, it'll take a while to get used to having him un-
derfoot. In fact, he's not a very likable man; there's something
murky and unpleasant about him. The one time Mrs. Eberhard brought him to visit, he sat in the living room and
seemed to regard everyone with detached curiosity, as if they
were all specimens on a dish under a lens. Brenda's grandfather had invited some old friends over from the bank—everyone was being careful not to let on that he wasn't still going
there every day. It was an awkward two hours, and Mrs. Eberhard's husband sat with his hands folded over his rounded
belly, his eyebrows arched. When he spoke, his voice was cultivated and quiet, full of self-satisfaction and haughtiness.
They had been speaking in low tones about how Jane Eberhard had moved in to take over after the accident, and Mrs.
Eberhard's husband cleared his throat, held his fist gingerly
to his mouth, pursed his lips, and began a soft-spoken, lec-
ture-like monologue about his belief that there's no such
thing as an accident. His considered opinion was that there
are subconscious explanations for everything. Apparently, he
thought he was entertaining everyone. He sat with one leg
crossed over the other and held forth in his calm, magisterial
voice, explaining how everything can be reduced to a matter
of conscious or subconscious will. Finally his wife asked him
to let it alone, please, drop the subject.

"For example," he went on, "there are many collisions on

the highway in which no one appears to have applied brakes before impact, as if something in the victims had decided on death. And of course there are the well-known cases of people stopped on railroad tracks, with plenty of time to get off, who simply do not move. Perhaps it isn't being frozen by the perception of one's fate but a matter of decision making, of will. The victim decides on his fate."

"I think we've had enough, now," Jane Eberhard said.

The inappropriateness of what he had said seemed to dawn on him then. He shifted in his seat and grew very quiet, and when the evening was over he took Brenda's grandfather by the elbow and apologized. But even in the apology there seemed to be a species of condescension, as if he were really only sorry for the harsh truth of what he had wrongly deemed it necessary to say. When everyone was gone, Brenda said, "I don't like that man."

"Is it because of what he said about accidents?" her grandfather asked.

She shook her head. "I just don't like him."

"It's not true, what he said, honey. An accident is an accident."

She said, "I know." But she would not return his gaze.

"Your mother wasn't very happy here, but she didn't want to leave us. Not even—you know, without . . . without knowing it or anything."

"He wears perfume," she said, still not looking at him.

"It's cologne. Yes, he does—too much of it."

"It smells," she said.

IN THE AFTERNOON HE WALKS over to the school. The sidewalks are crowded with children, and they all seem to recognize him. They carry their books and papers and their hair is windblown and they run and wrestle with each other in the yards. The sun's high and very hot, and most of the clouds have broken apart and scattered. There's still a fairly steady wind, but it's gentler now, and there's no coolness in it.

Brenda is standing at the first crossing street down the hill from the school. She's surrounded by other children yet seems separate from them somehow. She sees him and smiles. He waits on his side of the intersection for her to cross, and when she reaches him he's careful not to show any obvious affection, knowing it embarrasses her.

"How was your day?" he begins.

"Mr. Clayton tried to make me quit today."

He waits.

"I didn't get over," she says. "I didn't even get close."

"What did Mr. Clayton say?"

"Oh—you know. That it's not important. That kind of stuff."

"Well," he says gently, "*is* it so important?"

"I don't know." She kicks at something in the grass along the edge of the sidewalk—a piece of a pencil someone else had discarded. She bends, picks it up, examines it, and then drops it. This is exactly the kind of slow, daydreaming behavior that used to make him angry and impatient with her mother. They walk on. She's concentrating on the sidewalk before them, and they walk almost in step.

"I'm sure I could never do a thing like going over a vaulting horse when I was in school," he says.

"Did they have that when you were in school?"

He smiles. "It was hard getting everything into the caves.

But sure, we had that sort of thing. We were an advanced tribe. We had fire, too."

"Okay," she's saying, "okay, okay."

"Actually, with me, it was pull-ups. We all had to do pull-ups. And I just couldn't do them. I don't think I ever accomplished a single one in my life."

"I can't do pull-ups," she says.

"They're hard to do."

"Everybody in the fifth and sixth grades can get over the vaulting horse," she says.

HOW MUCH SHE REMINDS HIM of her mother. There's a certain mobility in her face, a certain willingness to assert herself in the smallest gesture of the eyes and mouth. She has her mother's green eyes, and now he tells her this. He's decided to try this. He's standing, quite shy, in her doorway, feeling like an intruder. She's sitting on the floor, one leg outstretched, the other bent at the knee. She tries to touch her forehead to the knee of the outstretched leg, straining, and he looks away.

"You know?" he says. "They're just the same color—just that shade of green."

"What was my grandmother like?" she asks, still straining.

"She was a lot like your mother."

"I'm never going to get married."

"Of course you will. Well, I mean—if you want to, you will."

"How come you didn't ever get married again?"

"Oh," he says, "I had a daughter to raise, you know."

She changes position, tries to touch her forehead to the other knee.

"I'll tell you, that mother of yours was enough to keep me busy. I mean, I called her double trouble, you know, because I always said she was double the trouble a son would have been. That was a regular joke around here."

"Mom was skinny and pretty."

He says nothing.

"Am I double trouble?"

"No," he says.

"Is that really why you never got married again?"

"Well, no one would have me, either."

"Mom said you liked it."

"Liked what?"

"Being a widow."

"Yes, well," he says.

"Did you?"

"All these questions," he says.

"Do you think about Grandmom a lot?"

"Yes," he says. "That's—you know, we remember our loved ones."

She stands and tries to touch her toes without bending her legs. "Sometimes I dream that Mom's yelling at you and you're yelling back."

"Oh, well," he says, hearing himself say it, feeling himself back down from something. "That's—that's just a dream. You know, it's nothing to think about at all. People who love each other don't agree sometimes—it's—it's nothing. And I'll bet these exercises are going to do the trick."

"I'm very smart, aren't I?"

He feels sick, very deep down. "You're the smartest little girl I ever saw."

"You don't have to come tonight if you don't want to," she

says. "You can drop me off if you want, and come get me when it's over."

"Why would I do that?"

She mutters. "*I* would."

"Then why don't we skip it?"

"Lot of good *that* would do," she says.

FOR DINNER THEY DRINK APPLE JUICE, and he gets her to eat two slices of dry toast. The apple juice is for energy. She drinks it slowly and then goes into her room to lie down, to conserve her strength. She uses the word *conserve,* and he tells her he's so proud of her vocabulary. She thanks him. While she rests, he does a few household chores, trying really just to keep busy. The week's newspapers have been piling up on the coffee table in the living room, the carpets need to be vacuumed, and the whole house needs dusting. None of it takes long enough; none of it quite distracts him. For a while he sits in the living room with a newspaper in his lap and pretends to be reading it. She's restless too. She comes back through to the kitchen, drinks another glass of apple juice, and then joins him in the living room, turns the television on. The news is full of traffic deaths, and she turns to one of the local stations that shows reruns of old situation comedies. They both watch *M*A*S*H* without really taking it in. She bites the cuticles of her nails, and her gaze wanders around the room. It comes to him that he could speak to her now, could make his way through to her grief—and yet he knows that he will do no such thing; he can't even bring himself to speak at all. There are regions of his own sorrow that he simply lacks the strength to explore, and so he sits there watching her restlessness, and at last it's time to go over to the school. Jane Eberhard makes a surprise visit, bearing a handsome good-luck card she's fashioned herself. She kisses Brenda, behaves exactly as if Brenda were going off to some dangerous, faraway place. She stands in the street and waves at them as they pull away, and Brenda leans out the window to shout goodbye. A moment later, sitting back and staring out at the dusky light, she says she feels a surge of energy, and he tells her she's way ahead of all the others in her class, knowing words like *conserve* and *surge*.

"I've always known them," she says.

It's beginning to rain again. Clouds have been rolling in from the east, and the wind shakes the trees. Lightning flickers on the other side of the clouds. Everything seems threatening, relentless. He slows down. There are many cars parked along both sides of the street. "Quite a turnout," he manages.

"Don't worry," she tells him brightly. "I still feel my surge of energy."

It begins to rain as they get out of the car, and he holds his sport coat like a cape to shield her from it. By the time they get to the open front doors, it's raining very hard. People are crowding into the cafeteria, which has been transformed into an arena for the event—chairs set up on four sides of the room as though for a wrestling match. In the center, at the end of the long, bright-red mat, are the vaulting horse and the mini-trampoline. The physical-education teacher, Mr. Clayton, stands at the entrance. He's tall, thin, scragglylooking, a boy really, no older than twenty-five.

"There's Mr. Clayton," Brenda says.

"I see him."

"Hello, Mr. Clayton."

Mr. Clayton is quite distracted, and he nods quickly, leans toward Brenda, and points to a doorway across the hall. "Go on ahead," he says. Then he nods at her grandfather.

"This is it," Brenda says.

Her grandfather squeezes her shoulder, means to find the best thing to tell her, but in the next confusing minute he's lost her; she's gone among the others and he's being swept along with the crowd entering the cafeteria. He makes his way along the walls behind the chairs, where a few other people have already gathered and are standing. At the other end of the room a man is speaking from a lectern about old business, new officers for the fall. Brenda's grandfather recognizes some of the people in the crowd. A woman looks at him and nods, a familiar face he can't quite place. She turns to look at the speaker. She's holding a baby, and the baby's staring at him over her shoulder. A moment later, she steps back to stand beside him, hefting the baby higher and patting its bottom.

"What a crowd," she says.

He nods.

"It's not usually this crowded."

Again, he nods.

The baby protests, and he touches the miniature fingers of one hand—just a baby, he thinks, and everything still to go through.

"How is—um . . . Brenda?" she says.

"Oh," he says, "fine." And he remembers that she was Brenda's kindergarten teacher. She's heavier than she was then, and her hair is darker. She has a baby now.

"I don't remember all my students," she says, shifting the

baby to the other shoulder. "I've been home now for eighteen months, and I'll tell you, it's being at the PTA meeting that makes me see how much I *don't* miss teaching."

He smiles at her and nods again. He's beginning to feel awkward. The man is still speaking from the lectern, a meeting is going on, and this woman's voice is carrying beyond them, though she says everything out of the side of her mouth.

"I remember the way you used to walk Brenda to school every morning. Do you still walk her to school?"

"Yes."

"That's so nice."

He pretends an interest in what the speaker is saying.

"I always thought it was so nice to see how you two got along together—I mean these days it's really rare for the kids even to know who their grandparents *are*, much less have one to walk them to school in the morning. I always thought it was really something." She seems to watch the lectern for a moment, and then speaks to him again, this time in a near whisper. "I hope you won't take this the wrong way or anything, but I just wanted to say how sorry I was about your daughter. I saw it in the paper when Brenda's mother. . . . Well. You know, I just wanted to tell you how sorry. When I saw it in the paper, I thought of Brenda, and how you used to walk her to school. I lost my sister in an automobile accident, so I know how you feel—it's a terrible thing. Terrible. An awful thing to have happen. I mean it's much too sudden and final and everything. I'm afraid now every time I get into a car." She pauses, pats the baby's back, then takes something off its ear. "Anyway, I just wanted to say how sorry I was."

"You're very kind," he says.

"It seems so senseless," she murmurs. "There's something so senseless about it when it happens. My sister went through a stop sign. She just didn't see it, I guess. But it wasn't a busy road or anything. If she'd come along one second later or sooner nothing would've happened. So senseless. Two people driving two different cars coming along on two roads on a sunny afternoon and they come together like that. I mean—what're the chances, really?"

He doesn't say anything.

"How's Brenda handling it?"

"She's strong," he says.

"I would've said that," the woman tells him. "Sometimes I think the children take these things better than the adults do. I remember when she first came to my class. She told everyone in the first minute that she'd come from Oregon. That she was living with her grandfather, and her mother was divorced."

"She was a baby when the divorce—when she moved here from Oregon."

This seems to surprise the woman. "Really," she says, low. "I got the impression it was recent for her. I mean, you know, that she had just come from it all. It was all very vivid for her, I remember that."

"She was a baby," he says. It's almost as if he were insisting on it. He's heard this in his voice, and he wonders if she has, too.

"Well," she says, "I always had a special place for Brenda. I always thought she was very special. A very special little girl."

The PTA meeting is over, and Mr. Clayton is now standing at the far door with the first of his charges. They're all lining up outside the door, and Mr. Clayton walks to the microphone to announce the program. The demonstration will commence with the mini-trampoline and the vaulting horse: a performance by the fifth- and sixth-graders. There will also be a break-dancing demonstration by the fourth-grade class.

"Here we go," the woman says. "My nephew's afraid of the mini-tramp."

"They shouldn't make them do these things," Brenda's grandfather says, with a passion that surprises him. He draws in a breath. "It's too hard," he says, loudly. He can't believe himself. "They shouldn't have to go through a thing like this."

"I don't know," she says vaguely, turning from him a little. He has drawn attention to himself. Others in the crowd are regarding him now—one, a man with a sparse red beard and wild red hair, looking at him with something he takes for agreement.

"It's too much," he says, still louder. "Too much to put on a child. There's just so much a child can take."

Someone asks gently for quiet.

The first child is running down the long mat to the mini-trampoline; it's a girl, and she times her jump perfectly, soars over the horse. One by one, other children follow. Mr. Clayton and another man stand on either side of the horse and help those who go over on their hands. Two or three go over without any assistance at all, with remarkable effortlessness and grace.

"Well," Brenda's kindergarten teacher says, "there's my nephew."

The boy hits the mini-tramp and does a perfect forward flip in the air over the horse, landing upright and then rolling forward in a somersault.

"Yea, Jack!" she cheers. "No sweat! Yea, Jackie boy!"

The boy trots to the other end of the room and stands with the others; the crowd is applauding. The last of the sixth-graders goes over the horse, and Mr. Clayton says into the microphone that the fifth-graders are next. It's Brenda who's next. She stands in the doorway, her cheeks flushed, her legs looking too heavy in the tights. She's rocking back and forth on the balls of her feet, getting ready. It grows quiet. Her arms swing slightly, back and forth, and now, just for a moment, she's looking at the crowd, her face hiding whatever she's feeling. It's as if she were merely curious as to who is out there, but he knows she's looking for him, searching the crowd for her grandfather, who stands on his toes, unseen against the far wall, stands there thinking his heart might break, lifting his hand to wave.

Design

The Reverend Tarmigian was not well. You could see it in his face—a certain hollowness, a certain blueness in the skin. His eyes lacked luster and brightness. He had a persistent dry, deep cough; he'd lost a lot of weight. And yet on this fine, breezy October day he was out on the big lawn in front of his church, raking leaves. Father Russell watched him from the window of his study, and knew that if he didn't walk over there and say something to him about it, this morning—like so many recent mornings—would be spent fretting and worrying about Tarmigian, seventy-two years old and out raking leaves in the windy sun. He had been planning to speak to the old man for weeks, but what could you say to a man like that? An institution in Point Royal, old Tarmigian had been pastor of the neighboring church—Faith Baptist, only a hundred or so yards away on the other side of Tallawaw Creek—for more than three decades. He referred to himself in conversation as the Reverend Fixture. He was a stooped, frail man with wrinkled blue eyes and fleecy blond hair that showed freckled scalp in the light; there were dimples in his cheeks. One of his favorite jokes—one of the many jokes he was fond of repeating—was that he had the eyes of a clown built above the natural curve of a baby's bottom. He'd touch the dimples and smile, saying a thing like that. And the truth was he tended to joke too much—even about the fact that he was apparently taxing himself beyond the dictates of good health for a man his age.

It seemed clear to Father Russell—who was all too often worried about his own health, though he was thirty years younger than Tarmigian—that something was driving the older man to these stunts of killing work: raking leaves all morning in the fall breezes; climbing on a ladder to clear drainspouts; or, as he had done one day last week, lugging a bag of mulch across the road and up the hill to the little cemetery where his wife lay buried, as if there weren't plenty of people within arm's reach on any Sunday who would have done it gladly for him (and would have just as gladly stood by while he said his few quiet prayers over the grave). His wife had been dead twenty years, he had the reverential respect of the whole countryside, but something was driving the man and, withal, there was often a species of amused cheerfulness about him almost like elation, as though he were keeping some wonderful secret.

It was perplexing; it violated all the rules of respect for one's own best interest. And today, watching him rake leaves, Father Russell determined that he would speak to him about it. He would simply confront him—broach the subject of health and express an opinion. Father Russell understood enough about himself to know that this concern would seem uncharacteristically personal on his part—it might even be misconstrued in some way—but as he put a jacket on and started out of his own church, it was with a small thrill of resolution. It was time to interfere, regardless of the age difference and regardless of the fact that it had been Father Russell's wish to find ways of avoiding the company of the older man.

Tarmigian's church was at the top of a long incline, across a stone bridge over Tallawaw Creek. It was a rigorous walk, even on a cool day, as this one was. The air was blue and cool in the mottled shade, and there were little patches of steam on the creek when the breezes were still. The Reverend Tarmigian stopped working, leaned on the handle of the rake and watched Father Russell cross the bridge.

"Well, just in time for coffee."

"I'll have tea," Father Russell said, a little out of breath from the walk.

"You're winded," said Tarmigian.

"And you're white as a sheet."

It was true. Poor Tarmigian's cheeks were pale as death. There were two blotches on them, like bruises—caused, Father Russell was sure, by the blood vessels that were straining to break in the old man's head. He indicated the trees all around, burnished-looking and still loaded with leaves, and even now dropping some of them, like part of an argument for the hopelessness of this task the old man had set for himself.

"Why don't you at least wait until they're finished?" Father Russell demanded.

"I admit, it's like emptying the ocean with a spoon." Tarmigian put his rake down and motioned for the other man to follow him. They went through the back door into the older man's tidy little kitchen, where Father Russell watched him fuss and worry, preparing the tea. When it was ready, the two men went into the study to sit among the books and talk. It was the old man's custom to take an hour every day in this book-lined room, though with this bad cold he'd contracted, he hadn't been up to much of anything recently. It was hard to maintain his old fond habits, he said. He felt too tired, or too sick. It was just an end-of-summer cold, of course, and Tarmigian dismissed it with a wave of his hand. Yet Father Russell had observed the weight loss, the coughing; and the old man was willing to admit that lately his appetite had suffered.

"I can't keep anything down," he said. "Sort of keeps me discouraged from trying, you know? So I shed the pounds. I'm sure when I get over this flu—"

"Medical science is advancing," said the priest, trying for sarcasm. "They have doctors now with their own offices and instruments. It's all advanced to a sophisticated stage. You can even get medicine for the flu."

"I'm fine. There's no need for anyone to worry."

Father Russell had seen denial before: indeed, he saw some version of it almost every day, and he had a rich understanding of the psychology of it. Yet Tarmigian's statement caused a surprising little clot of anger to form in the back of his mind and left him feeling vaguely disoriented, as if the older man's blithe neglect of himself were a kind of personal affront.

Yet he found, too, that he couldn't come right out and say what he had come to believe: that the old man was jeopardizing his own health. The words wouldn't form on his lips. So he drank his tea and searched for an opening—a way of getting something across about learning to relax a bit, learning to take it easy. There wasn't a lot to talk about beyond Tarmigian's anecdotes and chatter. The two men were not particularly close: Father Russell had come to his own parish from Boston only a year ago, believing this small Virginia township to be the accidental equivalent of a demotion (the assignment, coming really like the drawing of a ticket out of a hat, was less than satisfactory). He had felt almost immediately that the overfriendly, elderly clergyman next door was a bit too southern for his taste—though Tarmigian was obviously a man of broad experience, having served in missions overseas as a young man, and it was true that he possessed a kind of simple, happy grace. So while the priest had spent a lot of time in the first days trying to avoid him for fear of hurting his feelings, he had learned finally that Tarmigian was unavoidable, and had come to accept him as one of the mild irritations of the place in which he now found himself. He had even considered that the man had a kind of charm, was amusing and generous. He would admit that there had been times when he found himself surprised by a faint stir of gladness when the old man could be seen on the little crossing bridge, heading down to pay another of his casual visits as if there were nothing better to do than to sit in Father Russell's parlor and make jokes about himself.

The trouble now, of course, was that everything about the old man, including his jokes, seemed tinged with the something terrible that the priest feared was happening to him. And here Father Russell was, watching him cough, watching him hold up one hand as if to ward off anything in the way of advice or concern about it. The cough took him deep, so that he had to gasp to get his breath back; but then he cleared his throat, sipped more of the tea and, looking almost frightfully white around the eyes, smiled and said, "I have a good one for you, Reverend Russell. I had a couple in my congregation—I won't name them, of course—who came to me yesterday afternoon, claiming they were going to seek a divorce. You know how long they've been married? They've been married fifty-two years. Fifty-two years and they say they can't stand each other. I mean can't stand to be in the same room with each other."

Father Russell was interested in spite of himself—and in spite of the fact that the old man had again called him "Reverend." This would be another of Tarmigian's stories, or another of his jokes. The priest felt the need to head him off. "That cough," he said.

Tarmigian looked at him as if he'd merely said a number or recited a day's date.

"I think you should see a doctor about it."

"It's just a cold, Reverend."

"I don't mean to meddle," said the priest.

"Yes, well. I was asking what you thought about a married couple who can't stand to be in the same room together after fifty-two years."

Father Russell said, "I guess I'd have to say I have trouble believing that."

"Well, believe it. And you know what I said to them? I said we'd talk about it for a while. Counseling, you know."

Father Russell said nothing.

"Of course," said Tarmigian, "as you know, we permit divorce. Something about an English king wanting one badly enough to start his own church. Oh, that was long ago, of course. But we do allow it when it seems called for."

"Yes," Father Russell said, feeling beaten.

"You know, I don't think it's a question of either one of them being interested in anybody else. There doesn't seem to be any romance or anything—nobody's swept anybody off anybody's feet."

The priest waited for him to go on.

"I can't help feeling it's a bit silly." Tarmigian smiled, sipped the tea, then put the cup down and leaned back, clasping his hands behind his head. "Fifty-two years of marriage, and they want to untie the knot. What do you say, shall I send them over to you?"

The priest couldn't keep the sullen tone out of his voice. "I wouldn't know what to say to them."

"Well—you'd tell them to love one another. You'd tell them that love is the very breath of living or some such thing. Just as I did."

Father Russell muttered, "That's what I'd have to tell them, of course."

Tarmigian smiled again. "We concur."

"What was their answer?"

"They were going to think about it. Give themselves some

time to think, really. That's no joke, either." Tarmigian laughed, coughing. Then it was just coughing.

"That's a terrible cough," said the priest, feeling futile and afraid and deeply irritable. His own words sounded to him like something learned by rote.

"You know what I think I'll tell them if they come back?"

He waited.

"I think I'll tell them to stick it out anyway, with each other." Tarmigian looked at him and smiled. "Have you ever heard anything more absurd?"

Father Russell made a gesture, a wave of the hand, that he hoped the other took for agreement.

Tarmigian went on: "It's probably exactly right—probably exactly what they should do, and yet such odd advice to think of giving two people who've been together fifty-two years. I mean, when do you think the phrase 'sticking it out' would stop being applicable?"

Father Russell shrugged and Tarmigian smiled, seemed to be awaiting some reaction.

"Very amusing," said Father Russell.

But the older man was coughing again.

From the beginning there had been things Tarmigian said and did which unnerved the priest. Father Russell was a man who could be undone by certain kinds of boisterousness, and there were matters of casual discourse he simply would never understand. Yet often enough over the several months of their association, he had entertained the suspicion that Tarmigian was harboring a bitterness, and that his occasional mockery of himself was some sort of reaction to it, if it wasn't in fact a way of releasing it.

Now Father Russell sipped his tea and looked away out the window. Leaves were flying in the wind. The road was in blue shade, and the shade moved. There were houses beyond the hill, but from here everything looked like a wilderness.

"Well," Tarmigian said, gaining control of himself. "Do you know what my poor old couple say is their major complaint? Their major complaint is they don't like the same TV programs. Now, can you imagine a thing like that?"

"Look," the priest blurted out. "I see you from my study window—you're—you don't get enough rest. I think you should see a doctor about that cough."

Tarmigian waved this away. "I'm fit as a fiddle, as they say. Really."

"If it's just a cold, you know," said Father Russell, giving up. "Of course—" he could think of nothing else to say.

"You worry too much," Tarmigian said. "You know, you've got bags under your eyes."

TRUE.

In the long nights Father Russell lay with a rosary tangled in his fingers and tried to pray, tried to stop his mind from playing tricks on him: the matter of greatest faith was and had been for a very long time now that every twist or turn of his body held a symptom, every change signified the onset of disease. It was all waiting to happen to him, and the anticipation of it sapped him, made him weak and sick at heart. He had begun to see that his own old propensity for morbid anxiety about his health was worsening, and the daylight hours required all his courage. Frequently he thought of Tarmigian as though the old man were in some strange way a reflection of his secretly held, worst fear. He recalled the lovely sunny mornings of his first summer as a curate, when he was twenty-seven and fresh and the future was made of slow time. This was not a healthy kind of thinking. It was middle age, he knew. It was a kind of spiritual dryness he had been taught to recognize and contend with. Yet each morning his dazed wakening—from whatever fitful sleep the night had yielded him—was greeted with the pall of knowing that the aging pastor of the next-door church would be out in the open, performing some strenuous task as if he were in the bloom of health. When the younger man looked out the window, the mere sight of the other building was enough to make him sick with anxiety.

ON FRIDAY FATHER RUSSELL WENT to Saint Celia Hospital to attend to the needs of one of his older parishioners, who had broken her hip in a fall, and while he was there a nurse walked in and asked that he administer the sacrament of extreme unction to a man in the emergency room. He followed her down the hall and the stairs to the first floor, and while they walked she told him the man had suffered a heart attack, that he was already beyond help. She said this almost matter-of-factly, and Father Russell looked at the delicate curve of her ears, thinking about design. This was, of course, an odd thing to be contemplating at such a somber time, yet he cultivated the thought, strove to concentrate on it, gazing at the intricacy of the nurse's red-veined ear lobe. Early in his priesthood, he had taught himself to make his mind settle on other things during moments requiring him to look upon sickness and death—he had worked to foster a healthy appreciation of, and attention to, insignificant things which were out of the province of questions of eternity and salvation and the common doom. It was what he had always managed as a protection against too clear a memory of certain daily horrors—images that could blow through him in the night like the very winds of fright and despair—and if over the years it had mostly worked, it had recently been in the process of failing him. Entering the crowded emergency room, he was concentrating on the whorls of a young woman's ear as an instrument for hearing, when he saw Tarmigian sitting in one of the chairs near the television, his hand wrapped in a bandage, his pallid face sunk over the pages of a magazine.

Tarmigian looked up, then smiled, held up the bandaged hand. There wasn't time for the two men to speak. Father Russell nodded at him and went on, following the nurse, feeling strangely precarious and weak. He looked back over his shoulder at Tarmigian, who had simply gone back to reading the magazine, and then he was attending to what the nurse had brought him to see: she pulled a curtain aside to reveal a gurney with two people on it—a man and a woman of roughly the same late middle age—the woman cradling the man's head in her arms and whispering something to him.

"Mrs. Simpson," the nurse said, "here's the priest."

Father Russell stood there while the woman regarded him. She was perhaps fifty-five, with iron gray hair and small, round, wet eyes. "Mrs. Simpson," he said to her.

"He's my husband," she murmured, rising, letting the man's head down carefully. His eyes were open wide, as was his mouth. "My Jack. Oh, Jack. Jack."

Father Russell stepped forward and touched her shoulder, and she cried, staring down at her husband's face.

"He's gone," she said. "We were talking, you know. We were thinking about going down to see the kids. And he just put his head down. We were talking about how the kids never come to visit and we were going to surprise them."

"Mrs. Simpson," the nurse said, "would you like a sedative? Something to settle your nerves—"

This had the effect of convincing the poor woman about what had just taken place: the reality of it sank into her features as the color drained from them. "No," she said in a barely audible whisper, "I'm fine."

Father Russell began quickly to say the words of the sacrament, and she stood by him, gazing down at the dead man.

"I—I don't know where he is," she said. "He just put his head down." Her hands trembled over the cloth of her husband's shirt, which was open wide at the chest, and it was a moment before Father Russell understood that she was trying to button the shirt. But her hands were shaking too much. She patted the shirt down, then bowed her head and sobbed. Somewhere in the jangled apparatus of the room something was beeping, and he heard air rushing through pipes; everything was obscured in the intricacies of procedure. And then he was simply staring at the dead man's blank countenance, all sound and confusion and movement falling away from him. It was as though he had never looked at anything like this before; he remained quite still, in a profound quiet, for some minutes before Mrs. Simpson got his attention again. She had taken him by the wrist.

"Father," she was saying. "Father, he was a good man. God has taken him home, hasn't He?"

Father Russell turned to face the woman, to take her hands into his own and to whisper the words of hope.

"**I THINK SEEING YOU THERE**—at the hospital," he said to Tarmigian. "It upset me in an odd way."

"I cut my hand opening the paint jar," Tarmigian said. He was standing on a stepladder in the upstairs hallway of his rectory, painting the crown molding. Father Russell had walked out of his church in the chill of first frost and made his way across the little stone bridge and up the incline to the old man's door, had knocked and been told to enter, and entering, finding no one, had reached back and knocked again.

"Up here," came Tarmigian's voice.

And the priest had climbed the stairs in a kind of torpor, his heart beating in his neck and face. He had blurted out that he wasn't feeling right, hadn't slept at all well, and finally he'd begun to hint at what he could divine as to why. He was now sitting on the top step, hat in hand, still carrying with him the sense of the long night he had spent, lying awake in the dark, seeing not the dead face of poor Mrs. Simpson's husband but Tarmigian holding up the bandaged hand and smiling. The image had wakened him each time he had drifted toward sleep.

"Something's happening to me," he said now, unable to believe himself.

The other man reached high with the paint brush, concentrating. The ladder was rickety.

"Do you want me to hold the ladder?"

"Pardon me?"

"Nothing."

"Did you want to know if I wanted you to hold the ladder?"

"Well, do you?"

"You're worried I'll fall."

"I'd like to help."

"And did you say something is happening to you?"

Father Russell was silent.

"Forget the ladder, son."

"I don't understand myself lately," said the priest.

"Are you making me your confessor or something there, Reverend?"

"I—I can't—"

"Because I don't think I'm equipped."

"I've looked at the dead before," said Father Russell. "I've held the dying in my arms. I've never been very much afraid of it. I mean I've never been morbid."

"Morbidity is an indulgence."

"Yes, I know."

"Simply refuse to indulge yourself."

"I'm forty-three—"

"A difficult age, of course. You don't know whether you fit with the grown-ups or the children." Tarmigian paused to cough. He held the top step of the ladder with both hands, and his shoulders shook. Everything tottered. Then he stopped, breathed, wiped his mouth with the back of one hand.

Father Russell said, "I meant to say, I don't think I'm worried about myself."

"Well, that's good."

"I'm going to call and make you an appointment with a doctor."

"I'm fine. I've got a cold. I've coughed like this all my life."

"Nevertheless."

Tarmigian smiled at him. "You're a good man—but you're learning a tendency."

NO PEACE.

Father Russell had entered the priesthood without the sort of fervent sense of vocation he believed others had. In fact, he'd entertained serious doubts about it right up to the last year of seminary—doubts that, in spite of his confessor's reassurances to the contrary, he felt were more than the normal upsets of seminary life. In the first place, he had come to it against the wishes of his father, who had entertained dreams of a career in law for him; and while his mother applauded the decision, her own dream of grandchildren was visibly languishing in her eyes as the time for his final vows approached. Both parents had died within a month of each other during his last year of studies, and so there had been times when he'd had to contend with the added problem of an apprehension that he might unconsciously be learning to use his vocation as a form of refuge. But finally, nearing the end of his training, seeing the completion of the journey, something in him rejoiced, and he came to believe that this was what having a true vocation was: no extremes of emotion, no real perception of a break with the world, though the terms of his faith and the ancient ceremony that his training had prepared him to celebrate spoke of just that. He was even-tempered and confident, and when he was ordained, he set about the business of being a parish priest. There were matters to involve himself in, and he found that he could be energetic and enthusiastic about most of them. The life was satisfying in ways he hadn't expected, and if in his less confident moments some part of him entertained the suspicion that he was not progressing spiritually, he was also not the sort of man to go very deeply into such questions: there were things to do. He was not a contemplative. Or he hadn't been.

Something was shifting in his soul.

Nights were terrible. He couldn't even pray now. He stood at his rectory window and looked at the light in the old man's window, and his imagination presented him with the belief that he could hear the faint rattle of the deep cough, though he knew it was impossible across that distance. When he said the morning mass, he leaned down over the host and had to work to remember the words. The stolid, calm faces of his parishioners were almost ugly in their absurd confidence in him, their smiles of happy expectation and welcome. He took their hospitality and their care of him as his due, and felt waves of despair at the ease of it, the habitual taste and lure of it, while all the time his body was aching in ways that filled him with dread and reminded him of Tarmigian's ravaged features.

Sunday morning early, it began to rain. Someone called, then hung up before he could answer. He had been asleep; the loud ring at that hour had frightened him, changed his heartbeat. He took his own pulse, then stood at his window and gazed at the darkened shape of Tarmigian's church. That morning after the second mass, exhausted, miserable, filled with apprehension, he crossed the bridge in the rain, made his way up the hill and knocked on the old man's door. There wasn't any answer. He peered through the window on the porch and saw that there were dishes on the table in the kitchen, which was visible through the arched hallway off the living room. Tarmigian's Bible lay open on the arm of the easy chair. Father Russell knocked loudly and then walked around the building, into the church itself. It was quiet. The wind stirred outside and sounded like traffic whooshing by. Father Russell could feel his own heartbeat in the pit of his stomach. He sat down in the last pew of Tarmigian's church and tried to calm himself. Perhaps ten minutes went by, and then he heard voices. The old man was coming up the walk outside, talking to someone. Father Russell stood, thought absurdly of trying to hide, but then the door was opened and Tarmigian walked in, accompanied by an old woman in a white woolen shawl. Tarmigian had a big umbrella, which he shook down and folded, breathing heavily from the walk and looking, as always, even in the pall of his decline, amused by something. He hadn't seen Father Russell yet, though the old woman had. She nodded and smiled broadly, her hands folded neatly over a small black purse.

"Well," Tarmigian said. "To what do we owe this honor, Reverend?"

It struck Father Russell that they might be laughing at him. He dismissed this thought and, clearing his throat, said, "I—I wanted to see you." His own voice sounded stiffly formal and somehow foolish to him. He cleared his throat again.

"This is Father Russell," Tarmigian said loudly to the old woman. Then he touched her shoulder and looked at the priest. "Mrs. Aldenberry."

"God bless you," Mrs. Aldenberry said.

"Mrs. Aldenberry wants a divorce," Tarmigian murmured.

"Eh?" she said. Then, turning to Father Russell, "I'm hard of hearing."

"She wants her own television set," Tarmigian whispered.

"Pardon me?"

"And her own room."

"I'm hard of hearing," she said cheerfully to the priest. "I'm deaf as a post."

"Irritates her husband," Tarmigian said.

"I'm sorry," said the woman, "I can't hear a thing."

Tarmigian guided her to the last row of seats, and she sat down there, folded her hands in her lap. She seemed quite content, quite trustful, and the old minister, beginning to stutter into a deep cough, winked at Father Russell—as if to say this was all very entertaining. "Now," he said, taking the priest by the elbow, "Let's get to the flattering part of all this—you walking over here getting yourself all wet because you're worried about me."

"I just wanted to stop by," Father Russell said. He was almost pleading. The old man's face, in the dim light, looked appallingly bony and pale.

"Look at you," said Tarmigian. "You're shaking."

Father Russell could not speak.

"Are you all right?"

The priest was assailed by the feeling that the older man found him somehow ridiculous—and he remembered the initial sense he'd had, when Tarmigian and Mrs. Aldenberry had entered, that he was being laughed at. "I just wanted to see how you were doing," he said.

"I'm a little under the weather," Tarmigian said, smiling.

And it dawned on Father Russell, with the force of a physical blow, that the old man knew quite well he was dying.

Tarmigian indicated Mrs. Aldenberry with a nod of his head. "Now I have to attend to the depths of this lady's sorrow. You know, she says she should've listened to her mother and not married Mr. Aldenberry fifty-two years ago. She's revising her own history; she can't remember being happy in all that time, not now, not after what's happened. Now you think about that a bit. Imagine her standing in a room slapping her forehead and saying 'What a mistake!' Fifty-two years. Oops. A mistake. She's glad she woke up in time. Think of it! And I'll tell you, Reverend, I think she feels lucky."

Mrs. Aldenberry made a prim, throat-clearing sound, then stirred in her seat, looking at them.

"Well," Tarmigian said, straightening, wiping the smile from his face. He offered his hand to the priest. "Shake hands. No. Let's embrace. Let's give this poor woman an ecumenical thrill."

Father Russell shook hands, then walked into the old man's extended arms. It felt like a kind of collapse. He was breathing the odor of bay rum and talcum and something else, too, something indefinable and dark, and to his astonishment he found himself fighting back tears. The two men stood there while Mrs. Aldenberry watched, and Father Russell was unable to control the sputtering and trembling that took hold of him. When Tarmigian broke the embrace, the priest turned away, trying to compose himself. Tarmigian was coughing again.

"Excuse me," said Mrs. Aldenberry. She seemed quite tentative and upset.

Tarmigian held up one hand, still coughing, and his eyes had grown wide with the effort to breathe.

"Hot honey with a touch of lemon and whiskey," she said, to no one in particular. "Works like a charm."

Father Russell thought about how someone her age would indeed learn to feel that humble folk remedies were effective in stopping illness. It was logical and reasonable, and he was surprised by the force of his own resentment of her for it. He stood there wiping his eyes and felt his heart constrict with bitterness.

"Well," Tarmigian said, getting his breath back.

"Hot toddy," said Mrs. Aldenberry. "Never knew it to fail." She was looking from one to the other of the two men, her expression taking on something of the look of tolerance. "Fix you up like new," she said, turning her attention to the priest, who could not stop blubbering. "What's—what's going on here?"

Father Russell had a moment of sensing that everything Tarmigian had done or said over the past year was somehow freighted with this one moment, and it took him a few seconds to recognize the implausibility of such a thing: no one could have planned it, or anticipated it, this one seemingly aimless gesture of humor—out of a habit of humorous gestures, and from a brave old man sick to death—that could feel so much like health, like the breath of new life.

He couldn't stop crying. He brought out a handkerchief and covered his face with it, then wiped his forehead. It had grown quiet. The other two were gazing at him. He straightened, caught his breath. "Excuse me."

"No excuse needed," Tarmigian said, looking down. His smile seemed vaguely uncertain now, and sad. Even a little afraid.

"What is going on here?" the old woman wanted to know.

"Why, nothing at all out of the ordinary," Tarmigian said, shifting the small weight of his skeletal body, clearing his throat, managing to speak very loudly, very gently, so as to reassure her, but making certain, too, that she could hear him.

The Eyes of Love

This particular Sunday in the third year of their marriage, the Truebloods are leaving a gathering of the two families—a cookout at Kenneth's parents' that has lasted well into the night and ended with his father telling funny stories about being in the army in Italy just after the war. The evening has turned out to be exactly the kind of raucous, beery gathering Shannon said it would be, trying to beg off going. She's pregnant, faintly nauseous all the time, and she's never liked all the talk. She's heard the old man's stories too many times.

"They're good stories," Kenneth said that morning as she poured coffee for them both.

"I've heard every one of them at least twice," said Shannon. "God knows how many times your mother has heard them."

He said, "You might've noticed everybody laughing when he tells them, Shannon. Your father laughs until I start thinking about his heart."

"He just wants to be a part of the group."

"He chokes on it," Kenneth said, feeling defensive and oddly embarrassed, as if some unflattering element of his personality had been cruelly exposed. "Jesus, Shannon. Sometimes I wonder what goes through your mind."

"I just don't feel like listening to it all," she told him. "Does it have to be a statement of some kind if I don't go? Can't you just say I'm tired?"

"Your father and sisters are supposed to be there."

"Well, I'm pregnant—can't I be tired?"

"What do you think?" Kenneth asked her, and she shook her head, looking discouraged and caught. "It's just a cookout," he went on. "Cheer up—maybe no one will want to talk."

"That isn't what I mean, and you know it," she said.

NOW SHE ROLLS THE WINDOW DOWN on her side and waves at everybody. "See you," she calls as Kenneth starts the car. For a moment they are sitting in the roar and rattle of the engine, which backfires and sends up a smell of burning oil and exhaust. Everyone's joking and calling to them, and Kenneth's three brothers begin teasing about the battered Ford Kenneth lacks the money to have fixed. As always he feels a suspicion that their jokes are too much at his expense, home from college four years and still out of a job in his chosen field, there being no college teaching jobs to be had anywhere in the region. He makes an effort to ignore his own misgiving, and anyway most of what they say is obliterated by the noise. He races the engine, and everyone laughs. It's all part of the uproar of the end of the evening, and there's good feeling all around. The lawn is illuminated with floodlights from the top of the house, and Kenneth's father stands at the edge of the sidewalk with one arm over *her* father's broad shoulders. Both men are a little tight.

"Godspeed," Kenneth's father says, with a heroic wave.

"Good-bye," says Shannon's father.

The two men turn and start unsteadily back to the house, and the others, Kenneth's mother and brothers and Shannon's two younger sisters, are applauding and laughing at the dizzy progress they make along the walk. Kenneth backs out of the driveway, waves at them all again, honks the horn and pulls away.

Almost immediately his wife gives forth a conspicuous expression of relief, sighing deeply and sinking down in the seat. This makes him clench his jaw, but he keeps silent. The street winds among trees in the bright fan of his headlights; it's going to be a quiet ride home. He's in no mood to talk now. She murmurs something beside him in the dark, but he chooses to ignore it. He tries to concentrate on driving, staring out at the road as if alone. After a little while she puts the radio on, looks for a suitable station, and the noise begins to irritate him, but he says nothing. Finally she gives up, turns the radio off. The windshield is dotting with rain. They come to the end of the tree-lined residential street, and he pulls out toward the city. Here the road already shimmers with water, the reflected lights of shops and buildings going on into the closing perspective of brightnesses ahead.

"Are you okay to drive?" she asks.

"What?" he says, putting the wipers on.

"I just wondered. You had a few beers."

"I had three beers."

"You had a few."

"Three," he says. "And I didn't finish the last one. What're you doing, counting them now?"

"Somebody better count them."

"I had three goddamn beers," he says.

In fact, he hadn't finished the third beer because he'd begun to experience heartburn shortly after his father started telling the stories. He's sober all right, full of club soda and coffee, and he feels strangely lucid, as if the chilly night with its rain-smelling breezes has brought him wider awake, somehow. He puts both hands on the wheel and hunches forward slightly, meaning to ignore her shape, so quiet beside him. He keeps right at the speed limit, heading into the increasing rain, thinking almost abstractly about her.

"What're you brooding about?" she says.

The question surprises him. "I don't know," he says. "I'm driving."

"You're mad at me."

"No."

"Sure?" she asks.

"I'm sure."

WHAT HE IS SURE OF is that the day has been mostly ruined for him: the entire afternoon and evening spent in a state of vague tension, worrying about his wife's mood, wondering about what she might say or do or refuse to do in light of that mood. And the vexing thing is that toward the end, as he watched her watch his father tell the stories, the sense of something guilty began to stir in his soul, as if this were all something he had betrayed her into having to endure and there was something lurid or corrupt about it—an immoral waste of energy somehow, like a sort of spiritual gluttony. He's trying hard not to brood about it, but he keeps seeing her in the various little scenes played out during the course of the day—her watchfulness during his own clowning with his brothers and her quiet through the daylong chatter of simple observation and remarking that had gone on with her father and sisters, with Kenneth's parents. In each scene she seemed barely able to contain her weariness and boredom.

At one point while his father was basking in the laughter following a story about wine and a small boy in Rome who knew where the Germans had stored untold gallons of it, Kenneth stared at Shannon until she saw him, and when for his benefit she seemed discreetly to raise one eyebrow (it was just between them), her face, as she looked back at his father, took on a glow of tolerance along with the weariness it had worn—and something like affectionate exasperation, too.

Clearly she meant it as a gift to him, for when she looked at him again she smiled.

He might've smiled back. He had been laughing at something his father said. Again, though, he thought he saw the faintest elevation of one of her eyebrows.

This expression, and the slight nod of her head, reminded

him with a discomforting nostalgic stab (had they come so far from there?) of the look she had given him from the other side of noisy, smoky rooms in rented campus houses, when they were in graduate school and had first become lovers and moved with a crowd of radical believers and artists, people who were somehow most happy when they were wakeful and ruffled in the drugged hours before dawn—after the endless far-flung hazy discussions, the passionate sophomoric talk of philosophy and truth and everything that was wrong with the world and the beautiful changes everyone expected.

Someone would be talking, and Shannon would somehow confide in him with a glance from the other side of the room. There had been a thrill in receiving this look from her, since it put the two of them in cahoots; it made them secret allies in a kind of dismissal, a superiority reserved for the gorgeous and the wise. And this time he thought for a moment that she was intending the look, intending for him to think about those other days, before the job market had forced them to this city and part-time work for his father; before the worry over rent and the pregnancy had made everything of their early love seem quite dreamy and childish. He almost walked over to take her hand. But then a moment later she yawned deeply, making no effort to conceal her sleepiness, and he caught himself wishing that for the whole of the evening he could have managed not to look her way at all. With this thought in his mind, he did walk over to her. "I guess you want to go."

"For two hours," she said.

"You should've told me."

"I think I did."

"No," he said.

"I'm too tired to think," she told him.

NOW, DRIVING THROUGH THE RAINY NIGHT, he glances over at her and sees that she's simply staring out the passenger window, her hands open in her lap. He wants to be fair. He reminds himself that she's never been the sort of person who feels comfortable—or with whom one feels comfortable—at a party: something takes hold of her; she becomes objective and heavily intellectual, sees everyone as species, somehow, everything as behavior. A room full of people laughing and having a good innocent time is nevertheless a manifestation of some kind of pecking order to her: such a gathering means nothing more than a series of meaningful body languages and gestures, nothing more than the forms of competition, and, as she has told him on more than one occasion, she refuses to allow herself to be drawn in; she will not play social games. He remembers now that in their college days he considered this attitude of hers to be an element of her sharp intelligence, her wit. He had once considered that the two of them were above the winds of fashion, intellectual and otherwise; he had once been proud of this quirk of hers.

It's all more complicated than that now, of course. Now he knows she's unable to help the fear of being with people in congregation, that it's all a function of her having been refused affection when she was a child, of having been encouraged to compete with her many brothers and sisters for the attentions of her mother, who over the years has been in and out of mental institutions, and two of whose children, Shannon's older sisters, grew sexually confused in their teens and later underwent sex-change operations. They are now two older brothers. Shannon and Kenneth have made jokes about this, but the truth is, she comes from a tremendously unhappy family. The fact that she's managed to put a marriage together is no small accomplishment. She's fought to overcome the confusion and troubles of her life at home, and she's mostly succeeded. When her father finally divorced her mother, Shannon was the one he came to for support; it was Shannon who helped get him situated with the two younger sisters; and it was Shannon who forgave him all the excesses he had been driven to by the mad excesses of her mother. Shannon doesn't like to talk about what she remembers of growing up, but Kenneth often thinks of her as a little girl in a house where nothing is what it ought to be. He would say she has a right to her temperament, her occasional paranoia in groups of people—and yet for some time now, in spite of all efforts not to, he's felt only exasperation and annoyance with her about it.

As he has felt annoyance about several other matters: her late unwillingness to entertain; her lack of energy; and her reluctance to have sex. She has only begun to show slightly, yet she claims she feels heavy and unsexy. He understands this, of course, but it worries him that when they're sitting together quietly in front of the television set and she reaches over and takes his hand—a simple gesture of affection from a woman expecting a child—he finds himself feeling itchy and irritable, aware of the caress as a kind of abbreviation, an abridgement: she doesn't mean it as a prelude to anything. He wants to be loving and gentle through it all, and yet he can't get rid of the feeling that this state of affairs is what she secretly prefers.

WHEN SHE MOVES ON THE FRONT SEAT next to him, her proximity actually startles him.

"What?" she says.

"I didn't say anything."

"You jumped a little."

"No," he says.

"All right." She settles down in the seat again.

A moment later he looks over at her. He wants to have the sense of recognition and comfort he has so often had when gazing upon her. But her face looks faintly deranged in the bad light, and he sees that she's frowning, pulling something down into herself. Before he can suppress it, anger rises like a kind of heat in the bones of his face. "Okay, what is it?" he says.

"I wish I was in bed."

"You *didn't* say anything to me about going," he says.

"Would you have listened?"

"I would've listened, sure," he says. "What kind of thing to say is that?"

She's silent, staring out her window.

"Look," he says, "just exactly what is it that's bothering you?"

She doesn't answer right away. "I'm tired," she tells him without quite turning to look at him.

"No, really," he says. "I want to hear it. Come on, let it out."

Now she does turn. "I told you this morning. I just don't like hearing the same stories all the time."

"They aren't all the same," he says, feeling unreasonably angry.

"Oh, of course they are. God—you were asking for them. Your mother deserves a medal."

"I like them. Mom likes them. Everybody likes them. Your father and your sisters like them."

"Over and over," she mutters, looking away again. "I just want to go to sleep."

"You know what your problem is?" he says. "You're a *critic*. That's what your problem is. Everything is something for you to evaluate and *decide* on. Even me. Especially me."

"You," she says.

"Yes," he says. "Me. Because this isn't about my father at all. It's about us."

She sits staring at him. She's waiting for him to go on. On an impulse, wanting to surprise and upset her, he pulls the car into a 7-Eleven parking lot and stops.

"What're you doing?" she says.

He doesn't answer. He turns the engine off and gets out, walks through what he is surprised to find is a blowing storm across to the entrance of the store and in. It's noisy here—five teenagers are standing around a video game while another is rattling buttons and cursing. Behind the counter an old man sits reading a magazine and sipping from a steaming cup. He smiles as Kenneth approaches, and for some reason Kenneth thinks of Shannon's father, with his meaty red hands and unshaven face, his high-combed double crown of hair and missing front teeth. Shannon's father looks like the Ukrainian peasant farmer he's descended from on the un-Irish side of that family. He's a stout, dull man who simply watches and listens. He has none of the sharp expressiveness of his daughter, yet it seems to Kenneth that he is more friendly—even, somehow, more tolerant. Thinking of his wife's boredom as a kind of aggression, he buys a pack of cigarettes, though he and Shannon quit smoking more than a year ago. He returns to the car, gets in without looking at her, dries his hands on his shirt, and tears at the cigarette pack.

"Oh," she says. "Okay—great."

He pulls out a cigarette and lights it with the dashboard lighter. She's sitting with her arms folded, still hunched down in the seat. He blows smoke. He wants to tell her, wants to set her straight somehow; but he can't organize the words in his mind yet. He's too angry. He wants to smoke the cigarette and then measure everything out for her, the truth as it seems to be arriving in his heart this night: that she's manipulative and mean when she wants to be, that she's devious and self-absorbed and cruel of spirit when she doesn't get her way—looking at his father like that, as if there were something sad about being able to hold a room in thrall at the age of seventy-five. Her own father howling with laughter the whole time . . .

"When you're through with your little game, I'd like to go home," she says.

"Want a cigarette?" he asks.

"This is so childish, Kenneth."

"Oh?" he says. "How childish is it to sit and *sulk* through an entire party because people don't conform to your wishes and—well, Jesus, I'm sorry, I don't think I quite know what the hell you wanted from everybody today. Maybe you could fill me in on it a little."

"I want some understanding from you," she says, beginning to cry.

"Oh, no," says Kenneth. "You might as well cut that out.

I'm not buying that. Not the way you sat yawning at my father tonight as if he was senile or something and you couldn't even be bothered to humor him."

"*Humor* him. Is that what everyone's doing?"

"You know better than that, Shannon. Either that or you're blind."

"All right," she says. "That was unkind. Now I don't feel like talking anymore, so let's just drop it."

He's quiet a moment, but the anger is still working in him. "You know the trouble with you?" he says. "You don't see anything with love. You only see it with your *brain*."

"Whatever you say," she tells him.

"Everything's locked up in your *head*," he says, taking a long drag of the cigarette and then putting it out in the ashtray. He's surprised by how good he feels—how much in charge, armed with being right about her: he feels he's made a discovery, and he wants to hold it up into the light and let her look at it.

"God, Kenneth. I felt sick all day. I'm pregnant."

He starts the car. "You know those people that live behind us?" he says. The moment has become almost philosophical to him.

She stares at him with her wet eyes, and just now he feels quite powerful and happy.

"Do you?" he demands.

"Of course I do."

"Well, I was watching them the other day. The way he is with the yard—right? We've been making such fun of him all summer. We've been so *smart* about his obsession with weeds and trimming and the almighty grass."

"I guess it's really important that we talk about these people now," she says. "Jesus."

"I'm telling you something you need to hear," Kenneth says. "Goddammit."

"I don't want to hear it now," she says. "I've been listening to talk all day. I'm tired of talk."

And Kenneth is shouting at her. "I'll just say this and then I'll shut up for the rest of the goddamn year if that's what you want!"

She says nothing.

"I'm telling you about these people. The man was walking around with a little plastic baggie on one hand, picking up the dog's droppings. Okay? And his wife was trimming one of the shrubs. She was trimming one of the shrubs and I thought for a second I could feel what she was thinking. There wasn't anything in her face, but I was so *smart,* like we are, you know, Shannon. I was so smart about it that I knew what she was thinking. I was so *perceptive* about these people we don't even know. These people we're too snobbish to speak to."

"You're the one who makes fun of them," Shannon says.

"Let me finish," he says. "I saw the guy's wife look at him from the other side of the yard, and it was like I could hear the words in her mind: 'My God, he's picking up the dog droppings again. I can't stand it another minute.' You know? But that *wasn't* what she was thinking. Because she walked over in a little while and helped him—actually pointed out a couple of places he'd missed, for God's sake. And then the two of them walked into their house arm in arm with their dog droppings. You see what I'm saying, Shannon? That woman was looking at him with love. She didn't see what I saw—there wasn't any criticism in it."

"I'm not criticizing anyone," his wife tells him. "I'm tired. I need to go home and get some sleep."

"But you *were* criticizing," he says, pulling back out into traffic. "Everything you did was a criticism. Don't you think it shows? You didn't even try to stifle any of it."

"Who's doing the criticizing now?" she says. "Are you the only one who gets to be a critic?"

He turns down the city street that leads home. He's looking at the lights going off in the shining, rainy distances. Beside him, his pregnant wife sits crying. There's not much traffic, but he seems to be traveling at just the speed to arrive at each intersection when the light turns red. At one light they sit for what seems an unusually long time, and she sniffles. And quite abruptly he feels wrong; he thinks of her in the bad days of her growing up and feels sorry for her. "Okay," he says. "Look, I'm sorry."

"Just let's be quiet," she says. "Can we just be quiet? God, if I could just not have the sound of *talk* for a while."

The car idles roughly, and the light doesn't change. He looks at the green one two blocks away and discovers in himself the feeling that some momentous outcome hinges on that light staying green long enough for him to get through it. With a weird pressure behind his eyes, everything shifts toward some inner region of rage and chance and fright: it's as if his whole life, his happiness, depends on getting through that signal before it, too, turns red. He taps his palm on the steering wheel, guns the engine a little like a man at the starting line of a race.

"Honey," she says. "I didn't mean to hurt your feelings."

He doesn't answer. His own light turns green, and in the

next instant he's got the pedal all the way to the floor. They go roaring through the intersection, the tires squealing, the back of the car fishtailing slightly in the wetness. She's at his side, quiet, bracing in the seat, her hands out on the dash, and in the moment of knowing how badly afraid she is he feels strangely reconciled to her, at a kind of peace, speeding through the rain. He almost wishes something would happen, something final, watching the light ahead change to yellow, then to red. It's close, but he makes it through. He makes it through and then realizes she's crying, staring out, the tears streaming down her face. He slows the car, wondering at himself, holding on to the wheel with both hands, and at the next red light he comes to a slow stop. When he sees that her hands are now resting on her abdomen, he thinks of her pregnancy as if for the first time; it goes through him like a bad shock to his nerves. "Christ," he says, feeling sick. "I'm sorry."

The rain beats at the windows and makes gray, moving shadows on the inside of the car. He glances at her, then looks back at the road.

"Honey?" she says. The broken note in her voice almost makes him wince.

He says, "Don't, it's all right." He's sitting there looking through the twin half-circles of water the wipers make.

She sniffles again.

"Shannon," he says. "I didn't mean any of it." But his own voice sounds false to him, a note higher, somehow, and it dawns on him that he's hoarse from shouting. He thinks of the weekend mornings they've lain in bed, happy and warm, luxuriating in each other. It feels like something in the distant past to him. And then he remembers being awakened by the roar of the neighbor's power mower, the feeling of superiority he had entertained about such a man, someone obsessed with a lawn. He's thinking of the man now, that one whose wife sees whatever she sees when she looks at him, and perhaps she looks at him with love.

Shannon is trying to gain control of herself, sobbing and coughing. The light changes, but no one's behind him, and so he moves over in the seat and puts his arms around her. A strand of her hair tickles his jaw, a little discomfort he's faintly aware of. He sits very still, saying nothing, while in the corner of his vision the light turns yellow, then red again. She's holding on to him, and she seems to nestle slightly. When the light turns back to green, she gently pulls away from him.

"We better go," she says, wiping her eyes.

He sits straight, presses the accelerator pedal carefully, like a much older man. He wishes he were someone else, wishes something would change, and then is filled with a shivering sense of the meaning of such thoughts. He's driving on in the rain, and they are silent for a time. They're almost home.

"I'm just so tired," Shannon says finally.

"It's all right," he tells her.

"Sweet," she says.

The fight's over. They've made up. She reaches across and gives his forearm a little affectionate squeeze. He takes her hand and squeezes back. Then he has both hands on the wheel again. Their apartment house is in sight now, down the street to the left. He turns to look at her, his wife, here in the shadowed and watery light, and then he quickly looks back at the road. It comes to him like a kind of fright that in the little idle moment of his gaze some part of him was marking the unpleasant downturn of her mouth, the chiseled, too-sharp curve of her jaw—the whole, disheveled, vaguely tattered look of her—as though he were a stranger, someone unable to imagine what anyone, another man, other men, someone like himself, could see in her to love.

The Fireman's Wife

Jane's husband, Martin, works for the fire department. He's on four days, off three; on three, off four. It's the kind of shift work that allows plenty of time for sustained recreation, and during the off times Martin likes to do a lot of socializing with his two shift mates, Wally Harmon and Teddy Lynch. The three of them are like brothers: they bicker and squabble and compete in a friendly way about everything, including their common hobby, which is the making and flying of model airplanes. Martin is fanatical about it—spends way too much money on the two planes he owns, which are on the worktable in the garage, and which seem to require as much maintenance as the real article. Among the arguments between Jane and her husband—about money, lack of time alone together, and housework—there have been some about the model planes, but Jane can't say or do much without sounding like a poor sport: Wally's wife, Milly, loves watching the boys, as she calls them, fly their planes, and Teddy Lynch's ex-wife, before they were divorced, had loved the model planes too. In a way, Jane is the outsider here: Milly Harmon has known Martin most of his life, and Teddy Lynch was once point guard to Martin's power forward on their high school basketball team. Jane is relatively new, having come to Illinois from Virginia only two years ago, when Martin brought her back with him from his reserve training there.

This evening, a hot September twilight, they're sitting on lawn chairs in the dim light of the coals in Martin's portable grill, talking about games. Martin and Teddy want to play Risk, though they're already arguing about the rules. Teddy says that a European version of the game contains a wrinkle that makes it more interesting, and Martin is arguing that the game itself was derived from some French game.

"Well, go get it," Teddy says, "and I'll show you. I'll bet it's in the instructions."

"Don't get that out now," Jane says to Martin.

"It's too long," Wally Harmon says.

"What if we play cards," Martin says.

"Martin doesn't want to lose his bet," Teddy says.

"We don't have any bets, Teddy."

"Okay, so let's bet."

"Let's play cards," Martin says. "Wally's right. Risk takes too long."

"I feel like conquering the world," Teddy says.

"Oh, Teddy," Milly Harmon says. "Please shut up."

She's expecting. She sits with her legs out, holding her belly as though it were unattached, separate from her. The child will be her first, and she's excited and happy; she glows, as if she knows everyone's admiring her.

Jane thinks Milly is spreading it on a little thick at times: lately all she wants to talk about is her body and what it's doing.

"I had a dream last night," Milly says now. "I dreamed that I was pregnant. Big as a house. And I woke up and I was. What I want to know is, was that a nightmare?"

"How did you feel in the dream?" Teddy asks her.

"I said. Big as a house."

"Right, but was it bad or good?"

"How would you feel if you were big as a house?"

"Well, that would depend on what the situation was."

"The situation is, you're big as a house."

"Yeah, but what if somebody was chasing me? I'd want to be big, right?"

"Oh, Teddy, please shut up."

"I had a dream," Wally says. "A bad dream. I dreamed I died. I mean, you know, I was dead—and what was weird was that I was also the one who had to call Milly to tell her about it."

"Oh, God," Milly says. "Don't talk about this."

"It was weird. I got killed out at sea or something. Drowned, I guess. I remember I was standing on the deck of this ship talking to somebody about how it went down. And then I was calling Milly to tell her. And the thing is, I talked like a stranger would—you know, 'I'm sorry to inform you that your husband went down at sea.' It was weird."

"How did you feel when you woke up?" Martin says.

"I was scared. I didn't know who I was for a couple of seconds."

"Look," Milly says, "I don't want to talk about dreams."

"Let's talk about good dreams," Jane says. "I had a good dream. I was fishing with my father out at a creek—some creek that felt like a real place. Like if I ever really did go fishing with my father, this is where we would have fished when I was small."

"What?" Martin says after a pause, and everyone laughs.

"Well," Jane says, feeling the blood rise in her face and neck, "I never—my father died when I was just a baby."

"I dreamed I got shot once," Teddy says. "Guy shot me with a forty-five automatic as I was running downstairs. I fell and hit bottom, too. I could feel the cold concrete on the side of my face before I woke up."

Milly Harmon sits forward a little and says to Wally, "Honey, why did you have to tell about having a dream like that? Now *I'm* going to dream about it, I just know it."

"I think we all ought to call it a night," Jane says. "You guys have to get up at six o'clock in the morning."

"What're you talking about?" Martin says. "We're going to play cards, aren't we?"

"I thought we were going to play Risk," Teddy says.

"All right," Martin says, getting out of his chair. "Risk it is."

Milly groans, and Jane gets up and follows Martin into the house. "Honey," she says. "Not Risk. Come on. We'd need four hours at least."

He says over his shoulder, "So then we need four hours."

"Martin, I'm tired."

He's leaning up into the hall closet, where the games are stacked. He brings the Risk game down and turns, holding it in both hands like a tray. "Look, where do you get off, telling everybody to go home the way you did?"

She stands there staring at him.

"These people are our friends, Jane."

"I just said I thought we ought to call it a night."

"Well *don't* say—all right? It's embarrassing."

He goes around her and back out to the patio. The screen door slaps twice in the jamb. She waits a moment and then moves through the house to the bedroom. She brushes her hair, thinks about getting out of her clothes. Martin's uniforms are lying across the foot of the bed. She picks them up, walks into the living room with them and drapes them over the back of the easy chair.

"Jane," Martin calls from the patio. "Are you playing or not?"

"Come on, Jane," Milly says. "Don't leave me alone out here."

"What color armies do you want?" Martin asks.

She goes to the patio door and looks out at them. Martin has lighted the tiki lamps; everyone's sitting at the picnic table in the moving firelight. "Come on," Martin says, barely concealing his irritation. She can hear it, and she wants to react to it—wants to let him know that she is hurt. But they're all waiting for her, so she steps out and takes her place at the table. She chooses green for her armies, and she plays the game to lose, attacking in all directions until her forces are so badly depleted that when Wally begins to make his own move she's the first to lose all her armies. This takes more than an hour. When she's out of the game, she sits for a while, cheering Teddy on against Martin, who is clearly going to win; finally she excuses herself and goes back into the house. The glow from the tiki lamps makes weird patterns on the kitchen wall. She pours herself a glass of water and drinks it down; then she pours more and swallows some aspirin. Teddy sees this as he comes in for more beer, and he grasps her by the elbow and asks if she wants something a little better than aspirin for a headache.

"Like what?" she says, smiling at him. She's decided a smile is what one offers under such circumstances; one laughs things off, pretends not to notice the glazed look in the other person's eyes.

Teddy is staring at her, not quite smiling. Finally he puts his hands on her shoulders and says, "What's the matter, lady?"

"Nothing," she says. "I have a headache. I took some aspirin."

"I've got some stuff," he says. "It makes America beautiful. Want some?"

She says, "Teddy."

"No problem," he says. He holds both hands up and backs away from her. Then he turns and is gone. She hears him begin to tease Martin about the French rules of the game. Martin is winning. He wants Wally Harmon to keep playing, and Wally wants to quit. Milly and Teddy are talking about flying the model airplanes. They know about an air show in Danville on Saturday. They all keep playing and talking, and for a long time Jane watches them from the screen door. She smokes half a pack of cigarettes, and she paces a little. She drinks three glasses of orange juice, and finally she walks into the bedroom and lies down with her face in her hands. Her forehead feels hot. She's thinking about the next four days, when Martin will be gone and she can have the house to herself. She hasn't been married even two years, and she feels crowded; she's depressed and tired every day. She never has enough time to herself. And yet when she's alone, she feels weak and afraid. Now she hears someone in the hallway and she sits up, smooths her hair back from her face. Milly Harmon comes in with her hands cradling her belly.

"Ah," Milly says. "A bed." She sits down next to Jane and then leans back on her hands. "I'm beat," she says.

"I have a headache," Jane says.

Milly nods. Her expression seems to indicate how unimportant she finds this, as if Jane had told her she'd already got over a cold or something. "They're in the garage now," she says.

"Who?"

"Teddy, Wally, Martin. Martin conquered the world."

"What're they doing?" Jane asks. "It's almost midnight."

"Everybody's going to be miserable in the morning," Milly says.

Jane is quiet.

"Oh," Milly says, looking down at herself. "He kicked. Want to feel it?"

She takes Jane's hand and puts it on her belly. Jane feels movement under her fingers, something very slight, like one heartbeat.

"Wow," she says. She pulls her hand away.

"Listen," Milly says. "I know we can all be overbearing

sometimes. Martin doesn't realize some of his responsibilities yet. Wally was the same way."

"I just have this headache," Jane says. She doesn't want to talk about it, doesn't want to get into it. Even when she talks to her mother on the phone and her mother asks how things are, she says it's all fine. She has nothing she wants to confide.

"You feel trapped, don't you," Milly says.

Jane looks at her.

"Don't you?"

"No."

"Okay—you just have a headache."

"I do," Jane says.

Milly sits forward a little, folds her hands over the roundness of her belly. "This baby's jumping all over the place."

Jane is silent.

"Do you believe my husband and that awful dream? I wish he hadn't told us about it—now I know I'm going to dream something like it. You know pregnant women and dreams. I begin to shake just thinking of it."

"Try not to think of it," Jane says.

Milly waits a moment and then clears her throat and says, "You know, for a while there after Wally and I were married, I thought maybe I'd made a mistake. I remember realizing that I didn't like the way he laughed. I mean, let's face it, Wally laughs like a hyena. And somehow that took on all kinds of importance—you know, I had to absolutely like everything about him or I couldn't like anything. Have you ever noticed the way he laughs?"

Jane has never really thought about it. But she says nothing now. She simply nods.

"But you know," Milly goes on, "all I had to do was wait. Just—you know, wait for love to come around and surprise me again."

"Milly, I have a headache. I mean, what do you think is wrong, anyway?"

"Okay," Milly says, rising.

Then Jane wonders whether the other woman has been put up to this conversation. "Hey," she says, "did Martin say something to you?"

"What would Martin say?"

"I don't know. I mean, I really don't know, Milly. Jesus Christ, can't a person have a simple headache?"

"Okay," Milly says. "Okay."

"I like the way everyone talks around me here, you know it?"

"Nobody's talking around you—"

"I think it's wonderful how close you all are."

"All right," Milly says, standing there with her hands folded under the bulge of her belly. "You just look so unhappy these days."

"Look," Jane says, "I have a headache, all right? I'm going to go to bed. I mean, the only way I can get rid of it is to lie down in the dark and be very quiet—okay?"

"Sure, honey," Milly says.

"So—goodnight, then."

"Right," Milly says. "Goodnight." She steps toward Jane and kisses her on the cheek. "I'll tell Martin to call it a night. I know Wally'll be miserable tomorrow."

"It's because they can take turns sleeping on shift," Jane says.

"I'll tell them," Milly says, going down the hall.

Jane steps out of her jeans, pulls her blouse over her head and crawls under the sheets, which are cool and fresh and crisp. She turns the light off and closes her eyes. She can't believe how bad it is. She hears them all saying goodnight, and she hears Martin shutting the doors and turning off the lights. In the dark she waits for him to get to her. She's very still, lying on her back with her hands at her sides. He goes into the bathroom at the end of the hall. She hears him cough, clear his throat. He's cleaning his teeth. Then he comes to the entrance of the bedroom and stands in the light of the hall.

"I know you're awake," he says.

She doesn't answer.

"Jane," he says.

She says, "What?"

"Are you mad at me?"

"No."

"Then what's wrong?"

"I have a headache."

"You always have a headache."

"I'm not going to argue now, Martin. So you can say what you want."

He moves toward her, is standing by the bed. He's looming above her in the dark. "Teddy had some dope."

She says, "I know. He offered me some."

"I'm flying," Martin says.

She says nothing.

"Let's make love."

"Martin," she says. Her heart is beating fast. He moves a little, staggers taking off his shirt. He's so big and quick and powerful; nothing fazes him. When he's like this, the feeling she has is that he might do anything. "Martin," she says.

"All right," he says. "I won't. Okay? You don't have to worry your little self about it."

"Look," she says.

But he's already headed into the hall.

"Martin," she says.

He's in the living room. He turns the television on loud. A rerun of *Kojak*. She hears Theo calling someone sweetheart. "Sweetheart," Martin says. When she goes to him, she finds that he's opened a beer and is sitting on the couch with his legs out. The beer is balanced on his stomach.

"Martin," she says. "You have to start your shift in less than five hours."

He holds the beer up. "Baby," he says.

IN THE MORNING HE'S SHEEPISH, obviously in pain. He sits at the kitchen table with his hands up to his head while she makes coffee and hard-boiled eggs. She has to go to work, too, at a car dealership in town. All day she sits behind a window with a circular hole in the glass, where people line up to pay for whatever the dealer sells or provides, including mechanical work, parts, license plates, used cars, rental cars and, of course, new cars. Her day is long and exhausting, and she's already feeling as though she worked all night. The booth she has to sit in is right off the service bay area, and the smell of exhaust and grease is everywhere. Everything seems coated with a film of grime. She's standing at her sink, looking at the sun coming up past the trees beyond her street, and without thinking about it she puts the water on and washes her hands. The idea of the car dealership is like something clinging to her skin.

"Jesus," Martin says. He can't eat much.

She's drying her hands on a paper towel.

"Listen," he says, "I'm sorry, okay?"

"Sorry?" she says.

"Don't press it, all right? You know what I mean."

"Okay," she says, and when he gets up and comes over to put his arms around her, she feels his difference from her. She kisses him. They stand there.

"Four days," he says.

When Teddy and Wally pull up in Wally's new pickup, she stands in the kitchen door and waves at them. Martin walks down the driveway, carrying his tote bag of uniforms and books to read. He turns around and blows her a kiss. This morning is like so many other mornings. They drive off. She goes back into the bedroom and makes the bed, and puts his dirty uniforms in the wash. She showers and chooses something to wear. It's quiet. She puts the radio on and then decides she'd rather have the silence. After she's dressed, she stands at the back door and looks out at the street. Children are walking to school in little groups of friends. She thinks about the four days ahead. What she needs is to get into the routine and stop thinking so much. She knows that problems in a marriage are worked out over time.

Before she leaves for work she goes out into the garage to look for signs of Teddy's dope. She doesn't want someone stumbling on incriminating evidence. On the worktable along the back wall are Martin's model planes. She walks over and stands staring at them. She stands very still, as if waiting for something to move.

AT WORK HER FRIEND EVELINE smokes one cigarette after another, apologizing for each one. During Martin's shifts Jane spends a lot of time with Eveline, who is twenty-nine and single and wants very much to be married. The problem is she can't find anyone. Last year, when Jane was first working at the dealership, she got Eveline a date with Teddy Lynch. Teddy took Eveline to Lum's for hot dogs and beer, and they had fun at first. But then Eveline got drunk and passed out—put her head down on her arms and went to sleep like a child asked to take a nap in school. Teddy put her in a cab for home and then called Martin to laugh about the whole thing. Eveline was so humiliated by the experience that she goes out of her way to avoid Teddy—doesn't want anything to do with him or with any of Martin's friends, or with Martin, for that matter. She will come over to the house only when she knows Martin is away at work. And when Martin calls the dealership and she answers the phone, she's very stiff and formal, and she hands the phone quickly to Jane.

Today things aren't very busy, and they work a crossword together, making sure to keep it out of sight of the salesmen, who occasionally wander in to waste time with them. Eveline plays her radio and hums along with some of the songs. It's a long, slow day, and when Martin calls Jane feels herself growing anxious—something is moving in the pit of her stomach.

"Are you still mad at me?" he says.

"No," she tells him.

"Say you love me."

"I love you."

"Everybody's asleep here," he says. "I wish you were with me."

She says, "Right."

"I do," he says.

"Okay."

"You don't believe me?"

"I said *okay*."

"Is it busy today?" he asks.

"Not too."

"You're bored, then."

"A little," she says.

"How's the headache?"

"Just the edge of one."

"I'm sorry," he says.

"It's not your fault."

"Sometimes I feel like it is."

"How's *your* head?" she says.

"Terrible."

"Poor boy."

"I wish something would happen around here," he says. "A lot of guys snoring."

"Martin," she says, "I've got to go."

"Okay."

"You want me to stop by tonight?" she asks.

"If you want to."

"Maybe I will."

"You don't have to."

She thinks about him where he is: she imagines him, comfortable, sitting on a couch in front of a television. Sometimes, when nothing's going on, he watches all the soaps. He was hooked on *General Hospital* for a while. That he's her husband seems strange, and she thinks of the nights she's lain in his arms, whispering his name over and over, putting her hands in his hair and rocking with him in the dark. She tells him she loves him, and hangs the phone up. Eveline makes a gesture of frustration and envy.

"Nuts," Eveline says. "Nuts to you and your lovey-dovey stuff."

Jane is sitting in a bath of cold inner light, trying to think of her husband as someone she recognizes.

"Let's do something tonight," Eveline says. "Maybe I'll get lucky."

"I'm not going with you if you're going to be giving strange men the eye," Jane says. She hasn't quite heard herself. She's surprised when Eveline reacts.

"How dare you say a nasty thing like that? I don't know if I want to go out with someone who doesn't think any more of me than *that*."

"I'm sorry," Jane says, patting the other woman's wrist. "I didn't mean anything by it, really. I was just teasing."

"Well, don't tease that way. It hurts my feelings."

"I'm sorry," Jane says again. "Please—really." She feels near crying.

"Well, okay," Eveline says. "Don't get upset. I'm half teasing myself."

Jane sniffles, wipes her eyes with the back of one hand.

"What's wrong, anyway?" Eveline says.

"Nothing," Jane says. "I hurt your feelings."

THAT EVENING THEY RIDE IN Eveline's car over to Shakey's for a pizza, and then stroll down to the end of the block, to the new mini-mall on Lincoln Avenue. The night is breezy and warm. A storm is building over the town square. They window-shop for a while, and finally they stop at a new corner café, to sit in a booth by the windows, drinking beer. Across the street one of the movies has ended, and people are filing out, or waiting around. A few of them head this way.

"They don't look like they enjoyed the movie very much," Eveline says.

"Maybe they did, and they're just depressed to be back in the real world."

"Look, what is it?" Eveline asks suddenly.

Jane returns her gaze.

"What's wrong?"

"Nothing."

"Something's wrong," Eveline says.

Two boys from the high school come past, and one of them winks at Jane. She remembers how it was in high school—the games of flirtation and pursuit, of ignoring some people and noticing others. That seemed like such an unbearable time, and it's already years ago. She watches Eveline light yet another cigarette and feels very much older than her own memory of herself. She sees the person she is now, with Martin, somewhere years away, happy, with children, and with different worries. It's a vivid daydream. She sits there fabricating it, feeling it for what it is and feeling, too, that nothing will change: the Martin she sees in the daydream is nothing like the man she lives with. She thinks of Milly Harmon, pregnant and talking about waiting to be surprised by love.

"I think I'd like to have a baby," she says. She hadn't known she would say it.

Eveline says, "Yuck," blowing smoke.

"Yuck," Jane says. "That's great. Great response, Evie."

They're quiet awhile. Beyond the square the clouds break up into tatters, and lightning strikes out. They hear thunder, and the smell of rain is in the air. The trees in the little park across from the theater move in the wind, and leaves blow out of them.

"Wouldn't you like to have a family?" Jane says.

"Sure."

"Well, the last time I checked, that meant having babies."

"Yuck," Eveline says again.

"Oh, all right—you just mean because of the pain and all."

"I mean yuck."

"Well, what does 'yuck' mean, okay?"

"What *is* the matter with you?" Eveline says. "What difference does it make?"

"I'm trying to have a normal conversation," Jane says, "and I'm getting these weird one-word answers, that's all. I mean what's 'yuck,' anyway? What's it mean?"

"Let's say it means I don't want to talk about having babies."

"I wasn't talking about you."

Each is now a little annoyed with the other. Jane has noticed that whenever she talks about anything that might border on plans for the future, the other woman becomes irritatingly sardonic and closemouthed. Eveline sits there smoking her cigarette and watching the storm come. From beyond the square they hear sirens, which seem to multiply. The whole city seems to be mobilizing. Jane thinks of Martin out there where all those alarms are converging. How odd to know where your husband is by a sound everyone hears. She remembers lying awake nights early in the marriage, hearing sirens and worrying about what might happen. And now, through a slanting sheet of rain, as though something in these thoughts has produced her, Milly Harmon comes, holding an open magazine above her head. She sees Jane and Eveline in the window and waves at them. "Oh, God," Eveline says. "Isn't that Milly Harmon?"

Milly comes into the café and stands for a moment, shaking water from herself. Her hair is wet, as are her shoulders. She pushes her hair away from her forehead, and wipes the rain away with the back of one hand. Then she walks over and says, "Hi, honey," to Jane, bending down to kiss her on the side of the face. Jane manages to seem glad to see her. "You remember my friend Eveline from work," she says.

"I think I do, sure," Milly says.

"Maybe not," Eveline says.

"No, I think I do."

"I have one of those faces that remind you of somebody you never met," Eveline says.

Jane covers this with a laugh as Milly settles on her side of the booth.

Milly is breathless, all bustle and worry, arranging herself, getting comfortable. "Do you hear that?" she says about the sirens. "I swear, it must be a big one. I wish I didn't hear the sirens. It makes me so jumpy and scared. Wally would never forgive me if I did, but I wish I could get up the nerve to go see what it is."

"So," Eveline says, blowing smoke, "how's the baby coming along?"

Milly looks down at herself. "Sleeping now, I think."

"Wally—is it Wally?"

"Wally, yes."

"Wally doesn't let you chase ambulances?"

"I don't chase ambulances."

"Well, I mean—you aren't allowed to go see what's what when you hear sirens?"

"I don't want to see."

"I guess not."

"He's seen some terrible things. They all have. It must be terrible sometimes."

"Right," Eveline says. "It must be terrible."

Milly waves her hand in front of her face. "I wish you wouldn't smoke."

"I was smoking before you came," Eveline says. "I didn't know you were coming."

Milly looks confused for a second. Then she sits back a little and folds her hands on the table. She's chosen to ignore Eveline. She looks at Jane and says, "I had that dream last night."

Jane says, "What dream?"

"That Wally was gone."

Jane says nothing.

"But it wasn't the same, really. He'd left me, you know—the baby was born and he'd just gone off. I was so mad at him. And I had this crying little baby in my lap."

Eveline swallows the last of her beer and then gets up and goes out to stand near the line of wet pavement at the edge of the awninged sidewalk.

"What's the matter with her?" Milly asks.

"She's just unhappy."

"Did I say something wrong?"

"No—really. It's nothing," Jane says.

She pays for the beer. Milly talks to her for a while, but Jane has a hard time concentrating on much of anything now, with sirens going and Eveline standing out there at the edge of the sidewalk. Milly goes on, talking nervously about Wally's leaving her in her dream and how funny it is that she woke up mad at him, that she had to wait a few minutes and get her head clear before she could kiss him good morning.

"I've got to go," Jane says. "I came in Eveline's car."

"Oh, I'm sorry—sure. I just stepped in out of the rain myself."

They join Eveline outside, and Milly says she's got to go get her nephews before they knock down the ice-cream parlor. Jane and Eveline watch her walk away in the rain, and Eveline says, "Jesus."

"She's just scared," Jane says. "God, leave her alone."

"I don't mean anything by it," Eveline says. "A little malice, maybe."

Jane says nothing. They stand there watching the rain and lightning, and soon they're talking about people at work, the salesmen and the boys in the parts shop. They're relaxed now; the sirens have stopped and the tension between them has lifted. They laugh about one salesman who's apparently interested in Eveline. He's a married man—an overweight, balding, middle-aged Texan who wears snakeskin boots and a string tie, and who has an enormous fake-diamond ring on the little finger of his left hand. Eveline calls him Disco Bill. And yet Jane thinks her friend may be secretly attracted to him. She teases her about this, or begins to, and then a clap of thunder so frightens them both that they laugh about it, off and on, through the rest of the evening. They wind up visiting Eveline's parents, who live only a block from the café. Eveline's parents have been married almost thirty years, and, sitting in their living room, Jane looks at their things—the love seat and the antique chairs, the handsome grandfather clock in the hall, the paintings. The place has a lovely *tended* look about it. Everything seems to stand for the kind of life she wants for herself: an attentive, loving husband; children; and a quiet house with a clock that chimes. She knows this is all very dreamy and childish, and yet she looks at Eveline's parents, those people with their almost thirty years' love, and her heart aches. She drinks four glasses of white wine and realizes near the end of the visit that she's talking too much, laughing too loudly.

IT'S VERY LATE when she gets home. She lets herself in the side door of the house and walks through the rooms, turning on all the lights, as is her custom—she wants to be sure no one is hiding in any of the nooks and crannies. Tonight she looks at everything and feels demeaned by it. Martin's clean uniforms are lying across the back of the lounge chair in the living room. The TV and the TV trays are in one corner, next to the coffee table, which is a gift from Martin's parents, something they bought back in the fifties, before Martin was born. Martin's parents live on a farm ten miles outside town, and for the past year Jane has had to spend Sundays out there, sitting in that living room with its sparse, starved look, listening to Martin's father talk about the weather, or what he had to eat for lunch, or the wrestling matches he watches on TV. He's a kindly man but he has nothing whatever of interest to say, and he seems to know it—his own voice always seems to surprise him at first, as if some profound inner silence had been broken; he pauses, seems to gather himself, and then continues with the considered, slow cadences of oration. He's tall and lean and powerful looking; he wears coveralls, and he reminds Jane of those pictures of hungry, bewildered men in the Dust Bowl thirties—with their sad, straight, combed hair and their desperation. Yet he's a man who seems quite certain about things, quite calm and satisfied. His wife fusses around him, making sure of his comfort, and he speaks to her in exactly the same soft, sure tones he uses with Jane.

Now, sitting in her own living room, thinking about this man, her father-in-law, Jane realizes that she can't stand another Sunday afternoon listening to him talk. It comes to her like a chilly premonition, and quite suddenly, with a kind of tidal shifting inside her, she feels the full weight of her unhappiness. For the first time it seems unbearable, like something that might drive her out of her mind. She breathes, swallows, closes her eyes and opens them. She looks at her own reflection in one of the darkened windows of the kitchen, and then she finds herself in the bedroom, pulling her things out of the closet and throwing them on the bed. Something about this is a little frantic, as though each motion fed some impulse to go further, go through with it—use this night, make her way somewhere else. For a long time she works, getting the clothes out where she can see them. She's lost herself in the practical matter of getting packed. She can't decide what to take, and then she can't find a suitcase or an overnight bag. Finally she settles on one of Martin's travel bags, from when he was in the reserves. She's hurrying, stuffing everything into the bag, and when the bag is almost full she stops, feeling spent and out of breath. She sits down at her dressing table for a moment, and now she wonders if perhaps this is all the result of what she's had to drink. The alcohol is wearing off. She has the beginning of a headache. But she knows that whatever she decides to do should be done in the light of day, not now, at night. At last she gets up from the chair and lies down on the bed to think. She's dizzy. Her mind swims. She can't think, so she remains where she is, lying in the tangle of clothes she hasn't packed yet. Perhaps half an hour goes by. She wonders how long this will go on. And then she's asleep. She's nowhere, not even dreaming.

SHE WAKES TO THE SOUND OF VOICES. She sits up and tries to get her eyes to focus, tries to open them wide enough to see in the light. The imprint of the wrinkled clothes is in the skin of her face; she can feel it with her fingers. And then she's watching as two men bring Martin in through the front door and help him lie down on the couch. It's all framed in the perspective of the hallway and the open bedroom door, and she's not certain that it's actually happening.

"Martin?" she murmurs, getting up, moving toward them. She stands in the doorway of the living room, rubbing her eyes and trying to clear her head. The two men are standing over her husband, who says something in a pleading voice to one of them. He's lying on his side on the couch, both hands bandaged, a bruise on the side of his face as if something had spilled there.

"Martin," Jane says.

And the two men move, as if startled by her voice. She realizes she's never seen them before. One of them, the younger one, is already explaining. They're from another company. "We were headed back this way," he says, "and we thought it'd be better if you didn't hear anything over the phone." While he talks, the older one is leaning over Martin, going on about insurance. He's a big square-shouldered man with an extremely rubbery look to his face. Jane notices this, notices the masklike quality of it, and she begins to tremble. Everything is oddly exaggerated—something is being said, they're telling her that Martin burned his hands, and another voice is murmuring something. Both men go on talking, apologizing, getting ready to leave her there. She's not fully awake. The lights in the room hurt her eyes; she feels a little sick to her stomach. The two men go out on the porch and then look back through the screen. "You take it easy, now," the younger one says to Jane. She closes the door, understands that what she's been hearing under the flow of the past few moments is Martin's voice muttering her name, saying something. She walks over to him.

"Jesus," he says. "It's awful. I burned my hands and I didn't even know it. I didn't even feel it."

She says, "Tell me what happened."

"God," he says. "Wally Harmon's dead. God. I saw it happen."

"Milly—" she begins. She can't speak.

He's crying. She moves to the entrance of the kitchen and turns to look at him. "I saw Milly tonight." The room seems terribly small to her.

"The Van Pickel Lumberyard went up. The warehouse. Jesus."

She goes into the kitchen and runs water. Outside the window above the sink she sees the dim street, the shadows of houses without light. She drinks part of a glass of water and then pours the rest down the sink. Her throat is still very dry. When she goes back into the living room, she finds him lying on his side, facing the wall.

"Martin?" she says.

"What?"

But she can't find anything to tell him. She says, "God— poor Milly." Then she makes her way into the bedroom and begins putting away the clothes. She doesn't hear him get up, and she's startled to find him standing in the doorway, staring at her.

"What're you doing?" he asks.

She faces him, at a loss—and it's her hesitation that gives him his answer.

"Jane?" he says, looking at the travel bag.

"Look," she tells him, "I had a little too much to drink tonight."

He just stares at her.

"Oh, this," she manages. "I—I was just going through what I have to wear."

But it's too late. "Jesus," he says, turning from her a little.

"Martin," she says.

"What."

"Does—did somebody tell Milly?"

He nods. "Teddy. Teddy stayed with her. She was crazy. Crazy."

He looks at his hands. It's as if he just remembered them. They're wrapped tight; they look like two white clubs. "Jesus, Jane, are you—" He stops, shakes his head. "Jesus."

"Don't," she says.

"Without even talking to me about it—"

"Martin, this is not the time to talk about anything."

He's quiet a moment, standing there in the doorway. "I keep seeing it," he says. "I keep seeing Wally's face. The—the way his foot jerked. His foot jerked like with electricity and he was—oh, Christ, he was already dead."

"Oh, don't," she says. "Please. Don't talk. Stop picturing it."

"They gave me something to make me sleep," he says.

"And I won't sleep." He wanders back into the living room. A few minutes later she goes to him there and finds that whatever the doctors gave him has worked. He's lying on his back, and he looks smaller somehow, his bandaged hands on his chest, his face pinched with grief, with whatever he's dreaming. He twitches and mutters something and moans. She turns the light off and tiptoes back to the bedroom. She's the one who won't sleep. She gets into the bed and huddles there, leaving the light on. Outside the wind gets up—another storm rolls in off the plains. She listens as the rain begins, and hears the far-off drumming of thunder. The whole night seems deranged. She thinks of Wally Harmon, dead out in the blowing, rainy dark. And then she remembers Milly and her bad dreams, how she looked coming from the downpour, the wet street, with the magazine held over her head—her body so rounded, so weighted down with her baby, her love, the love she had waited for, that she said had surprised her. These events are too much to think about, too awful to imagine. The world seems cruelly immense now, and remorselessly itself. When Martin groans in the other room, she wishes he'd stop, and then she imagines that it's another time, that she's just awakened from a dream and is trying to sleep while they all sit in her living room and talk the hours of the night away.

IN THE MORNING SHE'S AWAKE FIRST. She gets up and wraps herself in a robe and then shuffles into the kitchen and puts coffee on. For a minute it's like any other morning. She sits at the table to wait for the coffee water to boil. He comes in like someone entering a stranger's kitchen—his movements are tentative, almost shy. She's surprised to see that he's still in his uniform. He says, "I need you to help me go to the bathroom. I can't get my pants undone." He starts trying to work his belt loose.

"Wait," she says. "Here, hold on."

"I have to get out of these clothes, Jane. I think they smell like smoke."

"Let me do it," she says.

"Milly's in the hospital—they had to put her under sedation."

"Move your hands out of the way," Jane says to him.

She has to help with everything, and when the time comes for him to eat, she has to feed him. She spoons scrambled eggs into his mouth and holds the coffee cup to his lips, and when that's over with, she wipes his mouth and chin with a damp napkin. Then she starts bathwater running and helps him out of his underclothes. They work silently, and with a kind of embarrassment, until he's sitting down and the water is right. When she begins to run a soapy rag over his back, he utters a small sound of satisfaction and comfort. But then he's crying again. He wants to talk about Wally Harmon's death. He says he has to. He tells her that a piece of hot metal the size of an arrow dropped from the roof of the Van Pickel warehouse and hit poor Wally Harmon in the top of the back.

"It didn't kill him right away," he says, sniffling. "Oh, Jesus. He looked right at me and asked if I thought he'd be all right. We were talking about it, honey. He reached up—he—over his shoulder. He took ahold of it for a second. Then he—then he looked at me and said he could feel it down in his stomach."

"Don't think about it," Jane says.

"Oh, God." He's sobbing. "God."

"Martin, honey—"

"I've done the best I could," he says. "Haven't I?"

"Shhh," she says, bringing the warm rag over his shoulders and wringing it, so that the water runs down his back.

They're quiet again. Together they get him out of the tub, and then she dries him off, helps him into a pair of jeans.

"Thanks," he says, not looking at her. Then he says, "Jane."

She's holding his shirt out for him, waiting for him to turn and put his arms into the sleeves. She looks at him.

"Honey," he says.

"I'm calling in," she tells him. "I'll call Eveline. We'll go be with Milly."

"Last night," he says.

She looks straight at him.

He hesitates, glances down. "I—I'll try and do better." He seems about to cry again. For some reason this makes her feel abruptly very irritable and nervous. She turns from him, walks into the living room and begins putting the sofa back in order. When he comes to the doorway and says her name, she doesn't answer, and he walks through to the kitchen door.

"What're you doing?" she says to him.

"Can you give me some water?"

She moves into the kitchen and he follows her. She runs water, to get it cold, and he stands at her side. When the glass is filled, she holds it to his mouth. He swallows, and she takes the glass away. "If you want to talk about anything—" he says.

"Why don't you try to sleep awhile?" she says.

He says, "I know I've been talking about Wally—"

"Just please—go lie down or something."

"When I woke up this morning, I remembered everything, and I thought you might be gone."

"Well, I'm not gone."

"I knew we were having some trouble, Jane—"

"Just let's not talk about it now," she says. "All right? I have to go call Eveline." She walks into the bedroom, and when he comes in behind her she tells him very gently to please go get off his feet. He backs off, makes his way into the living room. "Can you turn on the television?" he calls to her.

She does so. "What channel do you want?"

"Can you just go through them a little?"

She's patient. She waits for him to get a good look at each channel. There isn't any news coverage; it's all commercials and cartoons and children's shows. Finally he settles on a rerun of *The Andy Griffith Show,* and she leaves him there. She fills the dishwasher and wipes off the kitchen table. Then she calls Eveline to tell her what's happened.

"You poor thing," Eveline says. "You must be so relieved. And I said all that bad stuff about Wally's wife."

Jane says, "You didn't mean it," and suddenly she's crying. She's got the handset held tight against her face, crying.

"You poor thing," Eveline says. "You want me to come over there?"

"No, it's all right—I'm all right."

"Poor Martin. Is he hurt bad?"

"It's his hands."

"Is it very painful?"

"Yes," Jane says.

LATER, WHILE HE SLEEPS ON THE SOFA, she wanders outside and walks down to the end of the driveway. The day is sunny and cool, with little cottony clouds—the kind of clear day that comes after a storm. She looks up and down the street. Nothing is moving. A few houses away someone has put up a flag, and it flutters in a stray breeze. This is the way it was, she remembers, when she first lived here—when she first stood on this sidewalk and marveled at how flat the land was, how far it stretched in all directions. Now she turns and makes her way back to the house, and then she finds herself in the garage. It's almost as if she's saying good-bye to everything, and as this thought occurs to her, she feels a little stir of sadness. Here on the worktable, side by side under the light from the one window, are Martin's model airplanes. He won't be able to work on them again for weeks. The light reveals the miniature details, the crevices and curves on which he lavished such care, gluing and sanding and painting. The little engines are lying on a paper towel at one end of the table; they smell just like real engines, and they're shiny with lubrication. She picks one of them up and turns it in the light, trying to understand what he might see in it that could require such time and attention. She wants to understand him. She remembers that when they dated, he liked to tell her about flying these planes, and his eyes would widen with excitement. She remembers that she liked him best when he was glad that way. She puts the little engine down, thinking how people change. She knows she's going to leave him, but just for this moment, standing among these things, she feels almost peaceful about it. There's no need to hurry. As she steps out on the lawn, she realizes she can take the time to think clearly about when and where; she can even change her mind. But she doesn't think she will.

He's up. He's in the hallway—he had apparently wakened and found her gone. "Jesus," he says. "I woke up and you weren't here."

"I didn't go anywhere," she says, and she smiles at him.

"I'm sorry," he says, starting to cry. "God, Janey, I'm so sorry. I'm all messed up here. I've got to go to the bathroom again."

She helps him. The two of them stand over the bowl. He's stopped crying now, though he says his hands hurt something awful. When he's finished he thanks her, and then tries a bawdy joke. "You don't have to let go so soon."

She ignores this, and when she has him tucked safely away, he says quietly, "I guess I better just go to bed and sleep some more if I can."

She's trying to hold on to the feeling of peace and certainty she had in the garage. It's not even noon, and she's exhausted. She's very tired of thinking about everything. He's talking about his parents; later she'll have to call them. But then he says he wants his mother to hear his voice first, to know he's all right. He goes on—something about Milly and her unborn baby, and Teddy Lynch—but Jane can't quite hear him: he's a little unsteady on his feet, and they have trouble negotiating the hallway together.

In their bedroom she helps him out of his jeans and shirt, and she actually tucks him into the bed. Again he thanks her. She kisses his forehead, feels a sudden, sick-swooning sense of having wronged him somehow. It makes her stand straighter, makes her stiffen slightly.

"Jane?" he says.

She breathes. "Try to rest some more. You just need to rest now." He closes his eyes and she waits a little. He's not asleep. She sits at the foot of the bed and watches him. Perhaps ten minutes go by. Then he opens his eyes.

"Janey?"

"Shhh," she says.

He closes them again. It's as if he were her child. She thinks of him as he was when she first saw him, tall and sure of himself in his uniform, and the image makes her throat constrict.

At last he's asleep. When she's certain of this, she lifts herself from the bed and carefully, quietly withdraws. As she closes the door, something in the flow of her own mind appalls her, and she stops, stands in the dim hallway, frozen in a kind of wonder: she had been thinking in an abstract way, almost idly, as though it had nothing at all to do with her, about how people will go to such lengths leaving a room— wishing not to disturb, not to awaken, a loved one.

Consolation

Late one summer afternoon, Milly Harmon and her older
sister, Meg, spend a blessed, uncomplicated hour at a
motel pool in Philadelphia, sitting in the shade of one of the
big umbrella tables. They drink tropical punch from cans, and
Milly nurses the baby, staring out at the impossibly silver ag-
itation of water around the body of a young, dark swimmer, a
boy with Spanish black hair and eyes. He's the only one in the
pool. Across the way, an enormous woman in a red terry-cloth
bikini lies on her stomach in the sun, her head resting on her

folded arms. Milly's sister puts her own head down for a moment, then looks at Milly. "I feel fat," she says, low. "I look like that woman over there, I just know it."

"Be quiet," Milly says. "Your voice carries."

"Nobody can hear us," Meg says. She's always worried about weight, though she's nothing like the woman across the way. Her thighs are heavy, her hips wide, but she's big-boned, as their mother always says; she's not built to be skinny. Milly's the one who's skinny. When they were growing up, Meg often called her "stick." Sometimes it was an endearment and sometimes it was a jibe, depending on the circumstances. These days, Meg calls her "honey" and speaks to her with something like the careful tones of sympathy. Milly's husband was killed last September, when Milly was almost six months pregnant, and the two women have traveled here to see Milly's in-laws, to show them their grandchild, whom they have never seen.

The visit hasn't gone well. Things have been strained and awkward. Milly is exhausted and discouraged, so her sister has worked everything out, making arrangements for the evening, preserving these few hours in the day for the two of them and the baby. In a way, the baby's the problem: Milly would never have suspected that her husband's parents would react so peevishly, with such annoyance, to their only grandson—the only grandchild they will ever have.

Last night, when the baby started crying at dinner, both the Harmons seemed to sulk, and finally Wally's father excused himself and went to bed—went into his bedroom and turned a radio on. His dinner was still steaming on his plate; they hadn't even quite finished passing the food around. The music sounded through the walls of the small house, while

Milly, Wally's mother and Meg sat through the meal trying to be cordial to each other, the baby fussing between them.

Finally Wally's mother said, "Perhaps if you nurse him."

"I just did," Milly told her.

"Well, he wants *something*."

"Babies cry," Meg put in, and the older woman looked at her as though she had said something off-color.

"Hush," Milly said to the baby. "Be quiet." Then there seemed nothing left to say.

Mrs. Harmon's hands trembled over the lace edges of the tablecloth. "Can I get you anything?" she said.

At the end of the evening she took Milly by the elbow and murmured, "I'm afraid you'll have to forgive us, we're just not used to the commotion."

"Commotion," Meg said as they drove back to the motel. "Jesus. Commotion."

Milly looked down into the sleeping face of her son. "My little commotion," she said, feeling tired and sad.

NOW MEG TURNS HER HEAD on her arms and gazes at the boy in the pool. "Maybe I'll go for a swim," she says.

"He's too young for you," Milly says.

Meg affects a forlorn sigh, then sits straight again. "You want me to take Zeke for a while?" The baby's name is Wally, after his dead father, but Meg calls him Zeke. She claims she's always called every baby Zeke, boy or girl, but she's especially fond of the name for *this* baby. This baby, she says, looks like a Zeke. Even Milly uses the name occasionally, as an endearment.

"He's not through nursing," Milly says.

It's been a hot day. Even now, at almost six o'clock, the sky is pale blue and crossed with thin, fleecy clouds that look like filaments of steam. Meg wants a tan, or says she does, but she's worn a kimono all afternoon, and hasn't moved out of the shade. She's with Milly these days because her marriage is breaking up. It's an amicable divorce; there are no children. Meg says the whole thing simply collapsed of its own weight. Neither party is interested in anyone else, and there haven't been any ugly scenes or secrets. They just don't want to be married to each other anymore, see no future in it. She talks about how civilized the whole procedure has been, how even the lawyers are remarking on it, but Milly thinks she hears some sorrow in her voice. She thinks of two friends of hers who have split up twice since the warehouse fire that killed Wally, and whose explanations, each time, have seemed to preclude any possibility of reconciliation. Yet they're now living together, and sometimes, when Milly sees them, they seem happy.

"Did I tell you that Jane and Martin are back together?" she asks Meg.

"Again?"

She nods.

"Tied to each other on a rock in space," Meg says.

"What?"

"Come on, let me hold Zeke." Meg reaches for the baby. "He's through, isn't he?"

"He's asleep."

Meg pretends to pout, extending her arm across the table and putting her head down again. She makes a yawning sound. "Where are all the boys? Let's have some fun here anyway—right? Let's get in a festive mood or something."

Milly removes the baby's tight little sucking mouth from

her breast and covers herself. The baby sleeps on, still sucking. "Look at this," she says to her sister.

Meg leans toward her to see. "What in the world do you think is wrong with them?"

She's talking about Wally's parents, of course. Milly shrugs. She doesn't feel comfortable discussing them. She wants the baby to have both sets of grandparents, and a part of her feels that this ambition is in some way laudatory—that the strange, stiff people she has brought her child all this way to see ought to appreciate what she's trying to do. She wonders if they harbor some resentment about how before she would marry their son she'd extracted a promise from him about not leaving Illinois, where her parents and her sister live. It's entirely possible that Wally's parents unconsciously blame her for Wally's death, for the fact that his body lies far away in her family's plot in a cemetery in Lincoln, Illinois.

"Hey," Meg says.

"What."

"I asked a question. You drove all the way out here to see them and let them see their grandson, and they act like it's some kind of bother."

"They're just tired," Milly says. "Like we are."

"Seven hundred miles of driving to sit by a motel pool."

"They're not used to having a baby around," Milly says. "It's awkward for them, too." She wishes her sister would stop. "Can't we just not worry it all to death?"

"Hey," Meg says. "It's your show."

Milly says, "We'll see them tonight and then we'll leave in the morning and that'll be that, okay?"

"I wonder what they're doing right now. You think they're

watching the four o'clock movie or something? With their only grandson two miles away in a motel?"

In a parking lot in front of a group of low buildings on the other side of the highway, someone sets off a pack of fire-crackers—they make a sound like small machine-gun fire.

"All these years of independence," Meg says. "So people like us can have these wonderful private lives."

Milly smiles. It's always been Meg who defined things, who spoke out and offered opinions. Milly thinks of her sister as someone who knows the world, someone with experience she herself lacks, though Meg is only a little more than a year older. So much of her own life seems somehow duplicitous to her, as if the wish to please others and to be well thought of had somehow dulled the edges of her identity and left her with nothing but a set of received impressions. She knows she loves the baby in her lap, and she knows she loved her husband—though during the four years of her marriage she was confused much of the time, and afraid of her own restlessness. It was only in the weeks just before Wally was taken from her that she felt most comfortably in love with him, glad of his presence in the house and worried about the dangerous fire-fighting work that was, in fact, the agency of his death. She doesn't want to think about this now, and she marvels at how a moment of admiration for the expressiveness of her sister could lead to remembering that her husband died just as she was beginning to understand her need for him. She draws a little shuddering breath, and Meg frowns.

"You looked like something hurt you," Meg says. "You were thinking about Wally."

Milly nods.

"Zeke looks like him, don't you think?"

"I wasted so much time wondering if I loved him," Milly says.

"I think he was happy," her sister tells her.

In the pool the boy splashes and dives, disappears; Milly watches the shimmery surface. He comes up on the other side, spits a stream of water, and climbs out. He's wearing tight, dark blue bathing trunks.

"Come on," Meg says, reaching for the baby. "Let me have him."

"I don't want to wake him," Milly says.

Meg walks over to the edge of the pool, takes off her sandals, and dips the toe of one foot in, as though trying to gauge how cold the water is. She comes back, sits down, drops the sandals between her feet and steps into them one by one. "You know what I think it is with the Harmons?" she says. "I think it's the war. I think the war got them. That whole generation."

Milly ignores this, and adjusts, slightly, the weight of the baby in her lap. "Zeke," she says. "Pretty Zeke."

The big woman across the way has labored up off her towel and is making slow progress out of the pool area.

"Wonder if she's married," Meg says. "I think I'll have a pool party when the divorce is final."

The baby stirs in Milly's lap. She moves slightly, rocking her legs.

"We ought to live together permanently," Meg says.

"You want to keep living with us?"

"Sure, why not? Zeke and I get along. A divorced woman and a widow. And one cool baby boy."

They're quiet a while. Somewhere off beyond the trees at

the end of the motel parking lot, more firecrackers go off. Meg stands, stretches. "I knew a guy once who swore he got drunk and slept on top of the Tomb of the Unknown Soldier. On Independence Day. Think of it."

"You didn't believe him," Milly says.

"I believed he had the idea. Whole culture's falling apart. Whole goddamn thing."

"Do you really want to stay with us?" Milly asks her.

"I don't know. That's an idea, too." She ambles over to the pool again, then walks around it, out of the gate, to the small stairway leading up to their room. At the door of the room she turns, shrugs, seems to wait. Milly lifts the baby to her shoulder, then rises. Meg is standing at the railing on the second level, her kimono partway open at the legs. Milly, approaching her, thinks she looks wonderful, and tells her so.

"I was just standing here wondering how long it'll take to drive you crazy if we keep living together," Meg says, opening the door to the room. Inside, in the air-conditioning, she flops down on the nearest bed. Milly puts the baby in the Port-a-Crib and turns to see that the telephone message light is on. "Hey, look," she says.

Meg says, "Ten to one it's the Harmons canceling out."

"No bet," Milly says, tucking the baby in. "Oh, I just want to go home, anyway."

Her sister dials the front desk, then sits cross-legged with pillows at her back, listening. "I don't believe this," she says.

IT TURNS OUT THAT THERE ARE TWO CALLS: one from the Harmons, who say they want to come earlier than planned, and one from Meg's estranged husband, Larry, who has apparently traveled here from Champaign, Illinois. When Meg calls the number he left, he answers, and she waves Milly out of the room. Milly takes the baby, who isn't quite awake, and walks back down to the pool. It's empty; the water is perfectly smooth. She sits down, watches the light shift on the surface, clouds moving across it in reflection.

It occurs to her that she might have to spend the rest of the trip on her own, and this thought causes a flutter at the pit of her stomach. She thinks of Larry, pulling this stunt, and she wonders why she didn't imagine that he might show up, her sister's casual talk of the divorce notwithstanding. He's always been prone to the grand gesture: once, after a particularly bad quarrel, he rented a van with loudspeakers and drove up and down the streets of Champaign, proclaiming his love. Milly remembers this, sitting by the empty pool, and feels oddly threatened.

It isn't long before Meg comes out and calls her back. Meg is already trying to make herself presentable. What Larry wants, she tells Milly, what he pleaded for, is only that Meg agree to see him. He came to Philadelphia and began calling all the Harmons in the phone book, and when he got Wally's parents, they gave him the number of the motel. "The whole thing's insane," she says, hurriedly brushing her hair. "I don't get it. We're almost final."

"Meg, I need you now," Milly says.

"Don't be ridiculous," says her sister.

"What're we going to do about the Harmons?"

"Larry says they asked him to say hello to you. Can you feature that? I mean, what in the world is that? It's like they don't expect to see you again."

"Yes," Milly says. "But they're coming."

"He called before, you know."

"Mr. Harmon?"

"No—Larry. He called just before we left. I didn't get it. I mean, he kept hinting around and I just didn't get it. I guess I told him we were coming to Philly."

The baby begins to whine and complain.

"Hey, Zeke," Meg says. She looks in the mirror. "Good Lord, I look like war," and then she's crying. She moves to the bed, sits down, still stroking her hair with the brush.

"Don't cry," Milly says. "You don't want to look all red-eyed, do you?"

"What the hell," Meg says. "I'm telling you, I don't care about it. I mean—I don't care. He's such a baby about every-thing."

Milly is completely off balance. She has been the one in need on this trip, and now everything's turned around. "Here," she says, offering her sister a Kleenex. "You can't let him see you looking miserable."

"You believe this?" Meg says. "You think I should go with him?"

"He wants to take you somewhere?"

"I don't know."

"What about the Harmons?"

Meg looks at her. "What about them?"

"They're on their way here, too."

"I can't handle the Harmons anymore," Meg tells her.

"Who asked you to handle them?"

"You know what I mean."

"Well—are you just going to go off with Larry?"

"I don't know what he wants."

"Well, for God's sake, Meg. He wouldn't come all this way just to tell you hello."

"That's what he said. He said 'Hello.' "

"*Meg.*"

"I'm telling you, honey, I just don't have a clue."

IN A LITTLE WHILE LARRY ARRIVES, looking sheepish and expectant. Milly lets him in, and accepts his clumsy embrace, explaining that Meg is in the bathroom changing out of her bathing suit.

"Hey," he says, "I brought mine with me."

"She'll be through in a minute."

"Is she mad at me?" he asks.

"She's just changing," Milly tells him.

He looks around the room, walks over to the Port-a-Crib and stands there making little cooing sounds at the baby. "He's smiling at me. Look at that."

"He smiles a lot." She moves to the other side of the crib and watches him make funny faces at the baby.

Larry is a fair, willowy man, and though he's older than Milly, she has always felt a tenderness toward him for his obvious unease with her, for the way Meg orders him around, and for his boyish romantic fragility—which, she realizes now, reminds her a little of Wally. It's in the moment that she wishes he hadn't come here that she thinks of this, and abruptly she has an urge to reach across the crib and touch his wrist, as if to make up for some wrong she's done. He leans down and puts one finger into the baby's hand. "Look at that," he says. "Quite a grip. Boy's going to be a linebacker."

"He's small for his age," Milly tells him.

"It's not the size. It's the strength."

She says nothing. She wishes Meg would come out of the

bathroom. Larry pats the baby's forehead, then moves to the windows and, holding the drapes back, looks out.

"Pretty," he says. "Looks like it'll be a nice, clear night for fireworks."

For the past year or so, Larry has worked in a shoe store in Urbana, and he's gone through several other jobs, though he often talks about signing up for English courses at the junior college and getting started on a career. He wants to save money for school, but in five years he hasn't managed to save enough for one course. He explains himself in terms of his appetite for life: he's unable to put off the present, and frugality sometimes suffers. Meg has often talked about him with a kind of wonder at his capacity for pleasure. It's not a thing she would necessarily want to change. He can make her laugh, and he writes poems to her, to women in general, though according to Meg they're not very good poems.

The truth is, he's an amiable, dreamy young man without an ounce of objectivity about himself, and what he wears on this occasion seems to illustrate this. His bohemian dress is embarrassingly like a costume—the bright red scarf and black beret and jeans; the sleeveless turtleneck shirt, its dark colors bleeding into each other across the front.

"So," he says, turning from the windows. "Are the grandparents around?"

She draws in a breath, deciding to tell him about the Harmons, but Meg comes out of the bathroom at last. She's wearing the kimono open, showing the white shorts and blouse she's changed into.

Larry stands straight, clears his throat. "God, Meg. You look great," he says.

Meg flops down on the bed nearest the door and lights a cigarette. "Larry, what're you trying to pull here?"

"Nothing," he says. He hasn't moved. He's standing by the windows. "I just wanted to see you again. I thought Philadelphia on the Fourth might be good."

"Okay," Meg says, drawing on the cigarette.

"You know me," he says. "I have a hard time saying this sort of stuff up close."

"What sort of stuff, Larry."

"I'll take Zeke for a walk," Milly says.

"I can't believe this," Meg says, blowing smoke.

Milly gathers up the baby, but Larry stops her. "You don't have to go."

"Stay," Meg tells her.

"I thought I'd go out and meet the Harmons."

"Come on, tell me what you're doing here," Meg says to Larry.

"You don't know?"

"What if I need you to tell me anyway," she says.

He hesitates, then reaches into his jeans and brings out a piece of folded paper. "Here."

Meg takes it, but doesn't open it.

"Aren't you going to read it?"

"I can't read it with you watching me like that. Jesus, Larry—what in the world's going through your mind?"

"I started thinking about it being final," he says, looking down. Milly moves to the other side of the room, to her own bed, still holding the baby.

"I won't read it with you standing here," Meg says.

Larry reaches for the door. "I'll be outside," he says.

Milly, turning to sit with her back to them, hears the door

close quietly. She looks at Meg, who's sitting against the headboard of the other bed, the folded paper in her lap.

"Aren't you going to read it?"

"I'm embarrassed for him."

Milly recalls her own, secret, embarrassment at the unattractive, hyena-like note poor Wally struck every time he laughed. "It was probably done with love," she says.

Meg offers her the piece of paper across the space between the two beds. "You read it to me."

"I can't do that, Meg. It's private. I shouldn't even be here."

Meg opens the folded paper, and reads silently. "Jesus," she says. "Listen to this."

"Meg," Milly says.

"You're my sister. Listen. 'When I began to think our time was really finally up/ My chagrined regretful eyes lumbered tightly shut.' Lumbered, for God's sake."

Milly says nothing.

"My eyes lumbered shut."

And quite suddenly the two of them are laughing. They laugh quietly, or they try to. Milly sets Zeke down on his back, and pulls the pillows of the bed to her face in an attempt to muffle herself, and when she looks up she sees Meg on all fours with her blanket pulled over her head and, beyond her, Larry's faint shadow through the window drapes. He's pacing. He stops and leans on the railing, looking out at the pool.

"Shhh," Meg says, finally. "There's more." She sits straight, composes herself, pushes the hair back from her face, and holds up the now crumpled piece of paper. "Oh," she says. "Ready?"

"Meg, he's right there."

Meg looks. "He can't hear anything."

"Whisper," Milly says.

Meg reads. " 'I cried and sighed under the lids of these lonely eyes/ Because I knew I'd miss your lavish thighs.' "

For a few moments they can say nothing. Milly, coughing and sputtering into the cotton smell of the sheets, has a moment of perceiving, by contrast, the unhappiness she's lived with these last few months, how bad it has been—this terrible time—and it occurs to her that she's managed it long enough not to notice it, quite. Everything is suffused in an ache she's grown accustomed to, and now it's as if she's flying in the face of it all. She laughs more deeply than she ever has, laughs even as she thinks of the Harmons, and of her grief. She's woozy from lack of air and breath. At last she sits up, wipes her eyes with part of the pillowcase, still laughing. The baby's fussing, so she works to stop, to gain some control of herself. She realizes that Meg is in the bathroom, running water. Then Meg comes out and offers her a wet washcloth.

"I didn't see you go in there."

"Quiet," Meg says. "Don't get me started again."

Milly holds the baby on one arm. "I have to feed Zeke some more."

"So once more I don't get to hold him."

They look at each other.

"Poor Larry," Meg says. "Married to a philistine. But—just maybe—he did the right thing, coming here."

"You don't suppose he heard us."

"I don't suppose it matters if he did. He'd never believe we could laugh at one of his *poems*."

"Oh, Meg—that's so mean."

"It's the truth. There are some things, honey, that love just won't change."

Now it's as if they are both suddenly aware of another context for these words—both thinking about Wally. They gaze at each other. But then the moment passes. They turn to the window and Meg says, "Is Larry out there? What'll I tell him anyway?" She crosses the room and looks through the little peephole in the door. "God," she says, "the Harmons are here."

MRS. HARMON IS STANDING IN FRONT OF THE DOOR with Larry, who has apparently begun explaining himself. Larry turns and takes Meg by the arm as she and Milly come out. "All the way from Champaign to head it off," he says to Mrs. Harmon. "I hope I just avoided making the biggest mistake of my life."

"God," Meg says to him. "If only you had money." She laughs at her own joke. Mrs. Harmon steps around her to take the baby's hand. She looks up at Milly. "I'm afraid we went overboard," she says. "We went shopping for the baby."

Milly nods at her. There's confusion now: Larry and Meg are talking, seem about to argue. Larry wants to know what Meg thinks of the poem, but Milly doesn't hear what she says to him. Mrs. Harmon is apologizing for coming earlier than planned.

"It's only an hour or so," Milly says, and then wonders if that didn't sound somehow ungracious. She can't think of anything else to say. And then she turns to see Mr. Harmon laboring up the stairs. He's carrying a giant teddy bear with a red ribbon wrapped around its thick middle. He has it over his shoulder, like a man lugging a body. The teddy bear is bigger than he is, and the muscles of his neck are straining as he sets it down. "This is for Wally," he says with a smile that seems sad. His eyes are moist. He puts one arm around his wife's puffy midriff and says, "I mean—if it's okay."

"I don't want to be divorced," Larry is saying to Meg.

Milly looks at the Harmons, at the hopeful, nervous expressions on their faces, and then she tries to give them the satisfaction of her best appreciation: she marvels at the size and the softness of the big teddy, and she holds the baby up to it, saying, "See? See?"

"It's quite impractical, of course," says Mr. Harmon.

"We couldn't pass it up," his wife says. "We have some other things in the car."

"I don't know where we'll put it," says Milly.

"We can keep it here," Mrs. Harmon hurries to say. She's holding on to her husband, and her pinched, unhappy features make her look almost frightened. Mr. Harmon raises the hand that had been around her waist and lightly, reassuringly, clasps her shoulder. He stands there, tall and straight in that intentionally ramrod-stiff way of his—the stance, he would say, of an old military man, which happens to be exactly what he is. His wife stands closer to him, murmurs something about the fireworks going off in the distance. It seems to Milly that they're both quite changed; it's as if they've come with bad news and are worried about hurting her with more of it. Then she realizes what it is they are trying to give her, in what is apparently the only way they know how, and she remembers that they have been attempting to get used to the loss of their only child. She feels her throat constrict, and when Larry reaches for her sister, putting his long, boy's arms around Meg, it's as if this embrace is somehow the expression of what they all feel. The Harmons are gazing at the baby now. Still arm in arm.

"Yes," Milly tells them, her voice trembling. "Yes, of course. You—we could keep it here."

Meg and Larry are leaning against the railing, in their embrace. It strikes Milly that she's the only one of these people without a lover, without someone to stand with. She lifts the baby to her shoulder and looks away from them all, but only for a moment. Far off, the sky is turning dusky; it's getting near the time for rockets and exploding blooms of color.

"Dinner for everyone," Mr. Harmon says, his voice full of brave cheerfulness. He leans close to Milly, and speaks to the child. "And you, young fellow, you'll have to wait awhile."

"We'll eat at the motel restaurant and then watch the fireworks," says Mrs. Harmon. "We could sit right here on the balcony and see it all."

Meg touches the arm of the teddy bear. "Thing's as big as a *real* bear," she says.

"I feel like fireworks," Larry says.

"They put on quite a show," says Mr. Harmon. "There used to be a big field out this way—before they widened the street. Big field of grass, and people would gather—"

"We brought Wally here when he was a little boy," Mrs. Harmon says. "So many—such good times."

"They still put on a good show," Mr. Harmon says, squeezing his wife's shoulder.

Milly faces him, faces them, fighting back any sadness. In the next moment, without quite thinking about it, she steps forward slightly and offers her child to Mrs. Harmon. Mrs. Harmon tries to speak, but can't. Her husband clears his throat, lifts the big teddy bear as if to show it to everyone again. But he, too, is unable to speak. He sets it down, and seems momentarily confused. Milly lightly grasps his arm above the elbow, and steps forward to watch her mother-in-law cradle the baby. Mrs. Harmon makes a slight swinging motion, looking at her husband, and then at Milly. "Such a pretty baby," she says.

Mr. Harmon says, "A handsome baby."

Meg and Larry move closer. They all stand there on the motel balcony with the enormous teddy bear propped against the railing. They are quiet, almost shy, not quite looking at each other, and for the moment it's as if, like the crowds beginning to gather on the roofs of the low buildings across the street, they have come here only to wait for what will soon be happening in every quarter of the city of brotherly love.

Letter to the Lady
of the House

It's exactly twenty minutes to midnight, on this the eve of
my seventieth birthday, and I've decided to address you,
for a change, in writing—odd as that might seem. I'm perfectly aware of how many years we've been together, even if I
haven't been very good about remembering to commemorate
certain dates, certain days of the year. I'm also perfectly
aware of how you're going to take the fact that I'm doing this
at all, so late at night, with everybody due to arrive tomorrow,
and the house still unready. I haven't spent almost five

decades with you without learning a few things about you that I can predict and describe with some accuracy, though I admit that, as you put it, lately we've been more like strangers than husband and wife. Well, so if we are like strangers, perhaps there are some things I can tell you that you won't have already figured out about the way I feel.

Tonight, we had another one of those long, silent evenings after an argument (remember?) over pepper. We had been bickering all day, really, but at dinner I put pepper on my potatoes and you said that about how I shouldn't have pepper because it always upsets my stomach. I bothered to remark that I used to eat chili peppers for breakfast and if I wanted to put plain old ordinary black pepper on my potatoes, as I had been doing for more than sixty years, that was my privilege. Writing this now, it sounds far more testy than I meant it, but that isn't really the point.

In any case, you chose to overlook my tone. You simply said, "John, you were up all night the last time you had pepper with your dinner."

I said, "I was up all night because I ate green peppers. Not black pepper, but green peppers."

"A pepper is a pepper, isn't it?" you said. And then I started in on you. I got, as you call it, legal with you—pointing out that green peppers are not black pepper—and from there we moved on to an evening of mutual disregard for each other that ended with your decision to go to bed early. The grandchildren will make you tired, and there's still the house to do; you had every reason to want to get some rest, and yet I felt that you were also making a point of getting yourself out of proximity with me, leaving me to my displeasure, with another ridiculous argument settling between us like a fog.

So, after you went to bed, I got out the whiskey and started pouring drinks, and I had every intention of putting myself into a stupor. It was almost my birthday, after all, and—forgive this, it's the way I felt at the time—you had nagged me into an argument and then gone off to bed; the day had ended as so many of our days end now, and I felt, well, entitled. I had a few drinks, without any appreciable effect (though you might well see this letter as firm evidence to the contrary), and then I decided to do something to shake you up. I would leave. I'd make a lot of noise going out the door; I'd take a walk around the neighborhood and make you wonder where I could be. Perhaps I'd go check into a motel for the night. The thought even crossed my mind that I might leave you altogether. I admit that I entertained the thought, Marie. I saw our life together now as the day-to-day round of petty quarreling and tension that it's mostly been over the past couple of years or so, and I wanted out as sincerely as I ever wanted anything.

My God, I wanted an end to it, and I got up from my seat in front of the television and walked back down the hall to the entrance of our room to look at you. I suppose I hoped you'd still be awake so I could tell you of this momentous decision I felt I'd reached. And maybe you were awake: one of our oldest areas of contention being the noise I make—the feather-thin membrane of your sleep that I am always disturbing with my restlessness in the nights. All right. Assuming you were asleep and don't know that I stood in the doorway of our room, I will say that I stood there for perhaps five minutes, looking at you in the half-dark, the shape of your body under the blanket—you really did look like one of the girls when they were little and I used to stand in the doorway of their rooms; your illness last year made you so small again—and, as I said, I thought I had decided to leave you, for your peace as well as mine. I know you have gone to sleep crying, Marie. I know you've felt sorry about things and wished we could find some way to stop irritating each other so much.

Well, of course I didn't go anywhere. I came back to this room and drank more of the whiskey and watched television. It was like all the other nights. The shows came on and ended, and the whiskey began to wear off. There was a little rain shower. I had a moment of the shock of knowing I was seventy. After the rain ended, I did go outside for a few minutes. I stood on the sidewalk and looked at the house. The kids, with their kids, were on the road somewhere between their homes and here. I walked up to the end of the block and back, and a pleasant breeze blew and shook the drops out of the trees. My stomach was bothering me some, and maybe it was the pepper I'd put on my potatoes. It could just as well have been the whiskey. Anyway, as I came back to the house, I began to have the eerie feeling that I had reached the last night of my life. There was this small discomfort in my stomach, and no other physical pang or pain, and I am used to the small ills and side effects of my way of eating and drinking; yet I felt the sense of the end of things more strongly than I can describe. When I stood in the entrance of our room and looked at you again, wondering if I would make it through to the morning, I suddenly found myself trying to think what I would say to you if indeed this *were* the last time I would ever be able to speak to you. And I began to know I would write you this letter.

At least words in a letter aren't blurred by tone of voice, by the old aggravating sound of me talking to you. I began with this and with the idea that, after months of thinking about it, I would at last try to say something to you that wasn't colored by our disaffections. What I have to tell you must be explained in a rather roundabout way.

I've been thinking about my cousin Louise and her husband. When he died and she stayed with us last summer, something brought back to me what is really only the memory of a moment; yet it reached me, that moment, across more than fifty years. As you know, Louise is nine years older than I, and more like an older sister than a cousin. I must have told you at one time or another that I spent some weeks with her, back in 1933, when she was first married. The memory I'm talking about comes from that time, and what I have decided I have to tell you comes from that memory.

Father had been dead four years. We were all used to the fact that times were hard and that there was no man in the house, though I suppose I filled that role in some titular way. In any case, when Mother became ill there was the problem of us, her children. Though I was the oldest, I wasn't old enough to stay in the house alone, or to nurse her, either. My grandfather came up with the solution—and everybody went along with it—that I would go to Louise's for a time, and the two girls would go to stay with Grandfather. You'll remember that people did pretty much what that old man wanted them to do.

So we closed up the house, and I got on a train to Virginia. I was a few weeks shy of fourteen years old. I remember that I was not able to believe that anything truly bad would come of Mother's pleurisy, and was consequently glad of the opportunity it afforded me to travel the hundred miles south to Charlottesville, where cousin Louise had moved with her new husband only a month earlier, after her wedding. Because *we* traveled so much at the beginning, you never got to really know Charles when he was young—in 1933 he was a very tall, imposing fellow, with bright red hair and a graceful way of moving that always made me think of athletics, contests of skill. He had worked at the Navy Yard in Washington, and had been laid off in the first months of Roosevelt's New Deal. Louise was teaching in a day school in Charlottesville so they could make ends meet, and Charles was spending most of his time looking for work and fixing up the house. I had only met Charles once or twice before the wedding, but already I admired him and wanted to emulate him. The prospect of spending time in his house, of perhaps going fishing with him in the small streams of central Virginia, was all I thought about on the way down. And I remember that we did go fishing one weekend, that I wound up spending a lot of time with Charles, helping to paint the house and to run water lines under it for indoor plumbing. Oh, I had time with Louise, too—listening to her read from the books she wanted me to be interested in, walking with her around Charlottesville in the evenings and looking at the city as it was then. Or sitting on her small porch and talking about the family, Mother's stubborn illness, the children Louise saw every day at school. But what I want to tell you has to do with the very first day I was there.

I know you think I use far too much energy thinking about and pining away for the past, and I therefore know that I'm taking a risk by talking about this ancient history, and by trying to make you see it. But this all has to do with you and me, my dear, and our late inability to find ourselves in the same room together without bitterness and pain.

That summer, 1933, was unusually warm in Virginia, and the heat, along with my impatience to arrive, made the train almost unbearable. I think it was just past noon when it pulled into the station at Charlottesville, with me hanging out one of the windows, looking for Louise or Charles. It was Charles who had come to meet me. He stood in a crisp-looking seersucker suit, with a straw boater cocked at just the angle you'd expect a young, newly married man to wear a straw boater, even in the middle of economic disaster. I waved at him and he waved back, and I might've jumped out the window if the train had slowed even a little more than it had before it stopped in the shade of the platform. I made my way out, carrying the cloth bag my grandfather had given me for the trip—Mother had said through her rheum that I looked like a carpetbagger—and when I stepped down to shake hands with Charles I noticed that what I thought was a new suit was tattered at the ends of the sleeves.

"Well," he said. "Young John."

I smiled at him. I was perceptive enough to see that his cheerfulness was not entirely effortless. He was a man out of work, after all, and so in spite of himself there was worry in his face, the slightest shadow in an otherwise glad and proud countenance. We walked through the station to the street, and on up the steep hill to the house, which was a small clapboard structure, a cottage, really, with a porch at the end of a short sidewalk lined with flowers—they were marigolds, I think—and here was Louise, coming out of the house, her arms already stretched wide to embrace me. "Lord," she said. "I swear you've grown since the wedding, John." Charles took my bag and went inside.

"Let me look at you, young man," Louise said.

I stood for inspection. And as she looked me over I saw that her hair was pulled back, that a few strands of it had come loose, that it was brilliantly auburn in the sun. I suppose I was a little in love with her. She was grown, and married now. She was a part of what seemed a great mystery to me, even as I was about to enter it, and of course you remember how that feels, Marie, when one is on the verge of things—nearly adult, nearly old enough to fall in love. I looked at Louise's happy, flushed face, and felt a deep ache as she ushered me into her house. I wanted so to be older.

Inside, Charles had poured lemonade for us and was sitting in the easy chair by the fireplace, already sipping his. Louise wanted to show me the house and the backyard—which she had tilled and turned into a small vegetable garden—but she must've sensed how thirsty I was, and so she asked me to sit down and have a cool drink before she showed me the upstairs. Now, of course, looking back on it, I remember that those rooms she was so anxious to show me were meager indeed. They were not much bigger than closets, really, and the paint was faded and dull; the furniture she'd arranged so artfully was coming apart; the pictures she'd put on the walls were prints she'd cut out—magazine covers, mostly—and the curtains over the windows were the same ones that had hung in her childhood bedroom for twenty years. ("Recognize these?" she said with a deprecating smile.) Of course, the quality of her pride had nothing to do with the fineness—or lack of it—in these things, but in the fact that they belonged to her, and that she was a married lady in her own house.

On this day in July, in 1933, she and Charles were waiting for the delivery of a fan they had scrounged enough money to buy from Sears, through the catalogue. There were things they would rather have been doing, especially in this heat, and especially with me there. Monticello wasn't far away, the university was within walking distance, and without too much expense one could ride a taxi to one of the lakes nearby. They had hoped that the fan would arrive before I did, but since it hadn't, and since neither Louise nor Charles was willing to leave the other alone while traipsing off with me that day, there wasn't anything to do but wait around for it. Louise had opened the windows and shut the shades, and we sat in her small living room and drank the lemonade, fanning ourselves with folded parts of Charles's morning newspaper. From time to time an anemic breath of air would move the shades slightly, but then everything grew still again. Louise sat on the arm of Charles's chair, and I sat on the sofa. We talked about pleurisy and, I think, about the fact that Thomas Jefferson had invented the dumbwaiter, how the plumbing at Monticello was at least a century ahead of its time. Charles remarked that it was the spirit of invention that would make a man's career in these days. "That's what I'm aiming for, to be inventive in a job. No matter what it winds up being."

When the lemonade ran out, Louise got up and went into the kitchen to make some more. Charles and I talked about taking a weekend to go fishing. He leaned back in his chair and put his hands behind his head, looking satisfied. In the kitchen, Louise was chipping ice for our glasses, and she began singing something low, for her own pleasure, a barely audible lilting, and Charles and I sat listening. It occurred to me that I was very happy. I had the sense that soon I would be embarked on my own life, as Charles was, and that an attractive woman like Louise would be there with me. Charles yawned and said, "God, listen to that. Doesn't Louise have the loveliest voice?"

AND THAT'S ALL I HAVE FROM THAT DAY. I don't even know if the fan arrived later, and I have no clear memory of how we spent the rest of the afternoon and evening. I remember Louise singing a song, her husband leaning back in his chair, folding his hands behind his head, expressing his pleasure in his young wife's voice. I remember that I felt quite extraordinarily content just then. And that's all I remember.

But there are, of course, the things we both know: we know they moved to Colorado to be near Charles's parents; we know they never had any children; we know that Charles fell down a shaft at a construction site in the fall of 1957 and was hurt so badly that he never walked again. And I know that when she came to stay with us last summer she told me she'd learned to hate him, and not for what she'd had to help him do all those years. No, it started earlier and was deeper than that. She hadn't minded the care of him—the washing and feeding and all the numberless small tasks she had to perform each and every day, all day—she hadn't minded this. In fact, she thought there was something in her makeup that liked being needed so completely. The trouble was simply that whatever she had once loved in him she had stopped loving, and for many, many years before he died, she'd felt only suffocation when he was near enough to touch her, only irritation and anxiety when he spoke. She said all this, and then looked at me, her cousin, who had been fortunate enough to have children, and to be in love over time, and said, "John, how have you and Marie managed it?"

And what I wanted to tell you has to do with this fact—

that while you and I had had one of our whispering arguments only moments before, I felt quite certain of the simple truth of the matter, which is that whatever our complications, we *have* managed to be in love over time.

"Louise," I said.

"People start out with such high hopes," she said, as if I wasn't there. She looked at me. "Don't they?"

"Yes," I said.

She seemed to consider this a moment. Then she said, "I wonder how it happens."

I said, "You ought to get some rest." Or something equally pointless and admonitory.

As she moved away from me, I had an image of Charles standing on the station platform in Charlottesville that summer, the straw boater set at its cocky angle. It was an image I would see most of the rest of that night, and on many another night since.

I CAN ALMOST HEAR YOUR VOICE as you point out that once again I've managed to dwell too long on the memory of something that's past and gone. The difference is that I'm not grieving over the past now. I'm merely reporting a memory, so that you might understand what I'm about to say to you.

The fact is, we aren't the people we were even then, just a year ago. I know that. As I know things have been slowly eroding between us for a very long time; we are a little tired of each other, and there are annoyances and old scars that won't be obliterated with a letter—even a long one written in the middle of the night in desperate sincerity, under the influence, admittedly, of a considerable portion of bourbon whiskey, but nevertheless with the best intention and hope:

that you may know how, over the course of this night, I came to the end of needing an explanation for our difficulty. We have reached this—place. Everything we say seems rather aggravatingly mindless and automatic, like something one stranger might say to another in any of the thousand circumstances where strangers are thrown together for a time, and the silence begins to grow heavy on their minds, and someone has to say something. Darling, we go so long these days without having anything at all to do with each other, and the children are arriving tomorrow, and once more we'll be in the position of making all the gestures that give them back their parents as they think their parents are, and what I wanted to say to you, what came to me as I thought about Louise and Charles on that day so long ago, when they were young and so obviously glad of each other, and I looked at them and knew it and was happy—what came to me was that even the harsh things that happened to them, even the years of anger and silence, even the disappointment and the bitterness and the wanting not to be in the same room anymore, even all that must have been worth it for such loveliness. At least I am here, at seventy years old, hoping so. Tonight, I went back to our room again and stood gazing at you asleep, dreaming whatever you were dreaming, and I had a moment of thinking how we were always friends, too. Because what I wanted finally to say was that I remember well our own sweet times, our own old loveliness, and I would like to think that even if at the very beginning of our lives together I had somehow been shown that we would end up here, with this longing to be away from each other, this feeling of being trapped together, of being tied to each other in a way that makes us wish for other times, some other place—I would have known enough to accept it all freely for the chance at that love. And if I could, I would do it all again, Marie. All of it, even the sorrow. My sweet, my dear adversary. For everything that I remember.

Aren't You Happy for Me?

"William Coombs, with two *o*'s," Melanie Ballinger told her father over long distance. "Pronounced just like the thing you comb your hair with. Say it."

Ballinger repeated the name.

"Say the whole name."

"I've got it, sweetheart. Why am I saying it?"

"Dad, I'm bringing him home with me. We're getting *married*."

For a moment, he couldn't speak.

"Dad? Did you hear me?"

"I'm here," he said.

"Well?"

Again, he couldn't say anything.

"Dad?"

"Yes," he said. "That's—that's some news."

"That's all you can say?"

"Well, I mean—Melanie—this is sort of quick, isn't it?" he said.

"Not that quick. How long did you and Mom wait?"

"I don't remember. Are you measuring yourself by that?"

"You waited six months, and you do too remember. And this is five months. And we're not measuring anything. William and I have known each other longer than five months, but we've been together—you know, as a couple— five months. And I'm almost twenty-three, which is two years older than Mom was. And don't tell me it was different when *you* guys did it."

"No," he heard himself say. "It's pretty much the same, I imagine."

"Well?" she said.

"Well," Ballinger said. "I'm—I'm very happy for you."

"You don't sound happy."

"I'm happy. I can't wait to meet him."

"Really? Promise? You're not just saying that?"

"It's good news, darling. I mean I'm surprised, of course. It'll take a little getting used to. The—the suddenness of it and everything. I mean, your mother and I didn't even know you were seeing anyone. But no, I'm—I'm glad. I can't wait to meet the young man."

"Well, and now there's something *else* you have to know."

"I'm ready," John Ballinger said. He was standing in the kitchen of the house she hadn't seen yet, and outside the window his wife, Mary, was weeding in the garden, wearing a red scarf and a white muslin blouse and jeans, looking young—looking, even, happy, though for a long while there had been between them, in fact, very little happiness.

"Well, this one's kind of hard," his daughter said over the thousand miles of wire. "Maybe we should talk about it later."

"No, I'm sure I can take whatever it is," he said.

The truth was that he had news of his own to tell. Almost a week ago, he and Mary had agreed on a separation. Some time for them both to sort things out. They had decided not to say anything about it to Melanie until she arrived. But now Melanie had said that she was bringing someone with her.

She was hemming and hawing on the other end of the line: "I don't know, see, Daddy, I—God. I can't find the way to say it, really."

He waited. She was in Chicago, where they had sent her to school more than four years ago, and where after her graduation she had stayed, having landed a job with an independent newspaper in the city. In March, Ballinger and Mary had moved to this small house in the middle of Charlottesville, hoping that a change of scene might help things. It hadn't; they were falling apart after all these years.

"Dad," Melanie said, sounding helpless.

"Honey, I'm listening."

"Okay, look," she said. "Will you promise you won't react?"

"How can I promise a thing like that, Melanie?"

"You're going to react, then. I wish you could just promise me you wouldn't."

"Darling," he said, "I've got something to tell you, too. Promise me *you* won't react."

She said "Promise" in that way the young have of being absolutely certain what their feelings will be in some future circumstance.

"So," he said. "Now, tell me whatever it is." And a thought struck through him like a shock. "Melanie, you're not—you're not pregnant, are you?"

She said, "How did you *know*?"

He felt something sharp move under his heart. "Oh, Lord. Seriously?"

"Jeez," she said. "Wow. That's really amazing."

"You're—*pregnant.*"

"Right. My God. You're positively clairvoyant, Dad."

"I really don't think it's a matter of any clairvoyance, Melanie, from the way you were talking. Are you—is it sure?"

"Of course it's sure. But—well, that isn't the really hard thing. Maybe I should just wait."

"Wait," he said. "Wait for what?"

"Until you get used to everything else."

He said nothing. She was fretting on the other end, sighing and starting to speak and then stopping herself.

"I don't know," she said finally, and abruptly he thought she was talking to someone in the room with her.

"Honey, do you want me to put your mother on?"

"No, Daddy. I wanted to talk to you about this first. I think we should get this over with."

"Get this over with? Melanie, what're we talking about here? Maybe I should put your mother on." He thought he might try a joke. "After all," he added, "I've never been pregnant."

"It's not about being pregnant. You *guessed* that."

He held the phone tight against his ear. Through the window, he saw his wife stand and stretch, massaging the small of her back with one gloved hand. *Oh, Mary.*

"Are you ready?" his daughter said.

"Wait," he said. "Wait a minute. Should I be sitting down? I'm sitting down." He pulled a chair from the table and settled into it. He could hear her breathing on the other end of the line, or perhaps it was the static wind he so often heard when talking on these new phones. "Okay," he said, feeling his throat begin to close. "Tell me."

"William's somewhat older than I am," she said. "There." She sounded as though she might hyperventilate.

He left a pause. "That's it?"

"Well, it's how much."

"Okay."

She seemed to be trying to collect herself. She breathed, paused. "This is even tougher than I thought it was going to be."

"You mean you're going to tell me something harder than the fact that you're pregnant?"

She was silent.

"Melanie?"

"I didn't expect you to be this way about it," she said.

"Honey, please just tell me the rest of it."

"Well, what did you mean by that, anyway?"

"Melanie, *you said* this would be hard."

Silence.

"Tell me, sweetie. Please?"

"I'm going to." She took a breath. "Dad, William's sixty—he's—he's sixty—sixty-three years old."

Ballinger stood. Out in the garden his wife had got to her knees again, pulling crabgrass out of the bed of tulips. It was a sunny near-twilight, and all along the shady street people were working in their little orderly spaces of grass and flowers.

"Did you hear me, Daddy? It's perfectly all right, too, because he's really a *young* sixty-three, and *very* strong and healthy, and look at George Burns."

"George Burns," Ballinger said. "George—George Burns?" Melanie, I don't understand."

"Come on, Daddy, stop it."

"No, what're you telling me?" His mind was blank.

"I said William is sixty-three."

"William who?"

"Dad. My fiancé."

"Wait, Melanie. You're saying your fiancé, the man you're going to marry, *he's* sixty-three?"

"A young sixty-three," she said.

"Melanie. Sixty-three?"

"Dad."

"You didn't say six feet three?"

She was silent.

"Melanie?"

"Yes."

"Honey, this is a joke, right? You're playing a joke on me."

"It is not a—it's not that. God," she said. "I don't believe this."

"You don't believe—" he began. "You don't believe—"

"Dad," she said. "I told you—" Again, she seemed to be talking to someone else in the room with her. Her voice trailed off.

"Melanie," he said. "Talk into the phone."

"I know it's hard," she told him. "I know it's asking you to take a lot in."

"Well, no," Ballinger said, feeling something shift inside, a quickening in his blood. "It's—it's a little more than that, Melanie, isn't it? I mean it's not a weather report, for God's sake."

"I should've known," she said.

"Forgive me for it," he said, "but I have to ask you something."

"It's all right, Daddy," she said as though reciting it for him. "I know what I'm doing. I'm not really rushing into anything—"

He interrupted her. "Well, good God, somebody rushed into something, right?"

"Daddy."

"Is that what you call *him*? No, *I'm* Daddy. You have to call him *Grand*daddy."

"That is *not* funny," she said.

"I wasn't being funny, Melanie. And anyway, that wasn't my question." He took a breath. "Please forgive this, but I have to know."

"There's nothing you really *have* to know, Daddy. I'm an adult. I'm telling you out of family courtesy."

"I understand that. Family courtesy exactly. Exactly, Melanie, that's a good phrase. Would you please tell me, out of family courtesy, if the baby is his."

"Yes." Her voice was small now, coming from a long way off.

"I am sorry for the question, but I have to put all this together. I mean you're asking me to take in a whole lot here, you know?"

"I said I understood how you feel."

"I don't think so. I don't think you quite understand how I feel."

"All right," she said. "I don't understand how you feel. But I think I knew how you'd react."

For a few seconds, there was just the low, sea sound of long distance.

"Melanie, have you done any of the math on this?"

"I should've bet money," she said in the tone of a person who has been proven right about something.

"Well, but Jesus," Ballinger said. "I mean he's older than *I* am, kid. He's—he's a *lot* older than I am." The number of years seemed to dawn on him as he spoke; it filled him with a strange, heart-shaking heat. "Honey, nineteen years. When he was my age, I was only two years older than you are now."

"I don't see what that has to do with anything," she said.

"Melanie, I'll be forty-five *all the way* in December. I'm a *young* forty-four."

"I know when your birthday is, Dad."

"Well, good God, this guy's nineteen years older than your own father."

She said, "I've grasped the numbers. Maybe you should go ahead and put Mom on."

"Melanie, you couldn't pick somebody a little closer to my age? Some snot-nosed forty-year-old?"

"Stop it," she said. "Please, Daddy. I know what I'm doing."

"Do you know how old he's going to be when your baby is ten? Do you? Have you given that any thought at all?"

She was silent.

He said, "How many children are you hoping to have?"

"I'm not thinking about that. Any of that. This is now, and I don't care about anything else."

He sat down in his kitchen and tried to think of something else to say. Outside the window, his wife, with no notion of what she was about to be hit with, looked through the patterns of shade in the blinds and, seeing him, waved. It was friendly, and even so, all their difficulty was in it. Ballinger waved back. "Melanie," he said, "do you mind telling me just where you happened to meet William? I mean how do you meet a person forty years older than you are. Was there a senior citizen–student mixer at the college?"

"Stop it, Daddy."

"No, I really want to know. If I'd just picked this up and read it in the newspaper, I think I'd want to know. I'd probably call the newspaper and see what I could find out."

"Put Mom on," she said.

"Just tell me how you met. You can do that, can't you?"

"Jesus Christ," she said, then paused.

Ballinger waited.

"He's a teacher, like you and Mom, only college. He was my literature teacher. He's a professor of literature. He knows everything that was ever written, and he's the most brilliant man I've ever known. You have no idea how fascinating it is to talk with him."

"Yes, and I guess you understand that over the years that's what you're going to be doing a *lot* of with him, Melanie. A lot of talking."

"I am carrying the proof that disproves *you*," she said.

He couldn't resist saying, "Did *he* teach you to talk like that?"

"I'm gonna hang up."

"You promised you'd listen to something *I* had to tell *you*."

"Okay," she said crisply. "I'm listening."

He could imagine her tapping the toe of one foot on the floor: the impatience of someone awaiting an explanation. He thought a moment. "He's a professor?"

"That's not what you wanted to tell me."

"But you said he's a professor."

"Yes, I said that."

"Don't be mad at me, Melanie. Give me a few minutes to get used to the idea. Jesus. Is he a professor emeritus?"

"If that means distinguished, yes. But I know what you're—"

"No, Melanie. It means *retired*. You went to college."

She said nothing.

"I'm sorry. But for God's sake, it's a legitimate question."

"It's a stupid, mean-spirited thing to ask." He could tell from her voice that she was fighting back tears.

"Is he there with you now?"

"Yes," she said, sniffling.

"Oh, Jesus Christ."

"Daddy, why are you being this way?"

"Do you think maybe we could've had this talk alone? What's he, listening on the other line?"

"No."

"Well, thank God for that."

"I'm going to hang up now."

"No, please don't hang up. Please let's just be calm and talk about this. We have some things to talk about here."

She sniffled, blew her nose. Someone held the phone for

her. There was a muffled something in the line, and then she was there again. "Go ahead," she said.

"Is he still in the room with you?"

"Yes." Her voice was defiant.

"Where?"

"Oh, for God's sake," she said.

"I'm sorry, I feel the need to know. Is he sitting down?"

"I *want* him here, Daddy. We both want to be here," she said.

"And he's going to marry you."

"Yes," she said impatiently.

"Do you think I could talk to him?"

She said something he couldn't hear, and then there were several seconds of some sort of discussion, in whispers. Finally she said, "Do you promise not to yell at him?"

"Melanie, he wants me to promise not to *yell* at him?"

"Will you promise?"

"Good God."

"Promise," she said. "Or I'll hang up."

"All right. I promise. I promise not to yell at him."

There was another small scuffing sound, and a man's voice came through the line. "Hello, sir." It was, as far as Ballinger could tell, an ordinary voice, slightly lower than baritone. He thought of cigarettes. "I realize this is a difficult—"

"Do you smoke?" Ballinger interrupted him.

"No, sir."

"All right. Go on."

"Well, I want you to know I understand how you feel."

"Melanie says she does, too," Ballinger said. "I mean I'm certain you both *think* you do."

"It was my idea that Melanie call you about this."

"Oh, really. That speaks well of you. You probably knew I'd find this a little difficult to absorb and that's why you waited until Melanie was pregnant, for Christ's sake."

The other man gave forth a small sigh of exasperation.

"So you're a professor of literature."

"Yes, sir."

"Oh, you needn't 'sir' me. After all, I mean I *am* the goddam kid here."

"There's no need for sarcasm, sir."

"Oh, I wasn't being sarcastic. That was a literal statement of this situation that obtains right here as we're speaking. And, really, Mr. . . . . It's Coombs, right?"

"Yes, sir."

"Coombs, like the thing you comb your hair with."

The other man was quiet.

"Just how long do you think it'll take me to get used to this? You think you might get into your seventies before I get used to this? And how long do you think it'll take my wife who's twenty-one years younger than you are to get used to this?"

Silence.

"You're too old for my *wife,* for Christ's sake."

Nothing.

"What's your first name again?"

The other man spoke through another sigh. "Perhaps we should just ring off."

"Ring off. Jesus. Ring off? Did you actually say 'ring off'? What're you, a goddam limey or something?"

"I am an American. I fought in Korea."

"Not World War One?"

The other man did not answer.

"How many other marriages have you had?" Ballinger asked him.

"That's a valid question. I'm glad you—"

"Thank you for the scholarly observation, *sir*. But I'm not sitting in a class. How many did you say?"

"If you'd give me a chance, I'd tell you."

Ballinger said nothing.

"Two, sir. I've had two marriages."

"Divorces?"

"I have been widowed twice."

"And—oh, I get it. You're trying to make sure that that never happens to you again."

"This is not going well at all, and I'm afraid I—I—" The other man stammered, then stopped.

"How did you expect it to go?" Ballinger demanded.

"Cruelty is not what I'd expected. I'll tell you that."

"You thought I'd be glad my daughter is going to be getting social security before I do."

The other was silent.

"Do you have any other children?" Ballinger asked.

"Yes, I happen to have three." There was a stiffness, an overweening tone, in the voice now.

"And how old are they, if I might ask."

"Yes, you may."

Ballinger waited. His wife walked in from outside, carrying some cuttings. She poured water in a glass vase and stood at the counter arranging the flowers, her back to him. The other man had stopped talking. "I'm sorry," Ballinger said. "My wife just walked in here and I didn't catch what you said. Could you just tell me if any of them are anywhere near my daughter's age?"

"I told you, my youngest boy is thirty-eight."

"And you realize that if *he* wanted to marry my daughter I'd be upset, the age difference there being what it is." Ballinger's wife moved to his side, drying her hands on a paper towel, her face full of puzzlement and worry.

"I told you, Mr. Ballinger, that I understood how you feel. The point is, we have a pregnant woman here and we both love her."

"No," Ballinger said. "That's not the point. The point is that you, sir, are not much more than a goddam statutory rapist. That's the point." His wife took his shoulder. He looked at her and shook his head.

"What?" she whispered. "Is Melanie all right?"

"Well, this isn't accomplishing anything," the voice on the other end of the line was saying.

"Just a minute," Ballinger said. "Let me ask you something else. Really now. What's the policy at that goddam university concerning teachers screwing their students?"

"Oh, my God," his wife said as the voice on the line huffed and seemed to gargle.

"I'm serious," Ballinger said.

"Melanie was not my student when we became involved."

"Is that what you call it? Involved?"

"Let me talk to Melanie," Ballinger's wife said.

"Listen," he told her. "Be quiet."

Melanie was back on the line. "Daddy? Daddy?"

"I'm here," Ballinger said, holding the phone from his wife's attempt to take it from him.

"Daddy, we're getting married and there's nothing you can do about it. Do you understand?"

"Melanie," he said, and it seemed that from somewhere far inside himself he heard that he had begun shouting at her. "Jee-zus good Christ. Your fiancé was almost *my* age *now* the day you were *born*. What the hell, kid. Are you crazy? Are you out of your mind?"

His wife was actually pushing against him to take the phone, and so he gave it to her. And stood there while she tried to talk.

"Melanie," she said. "Honey, listen—"

"Hang up," Ballinger said. "Christ. Hang it up."

"Please. Will you go in the other room and let me talk to her?"

"Tell her I've got friends. All these nice men in their forties. She can marry any one of my friends—they're babies. Forties—cradle fodder. Jesus, any one of them. Tell her."

"Jack, stop it." Then she put the phone against her chest. "Did you tell her anything about us?"

He paused. "That—no."

She turned from him. "Melanie, honey. What is this? Tell me, please."

He left her there, walked through the living room to the hall and back around to the kitchen. He was all nervous energy, crazy with it, pacing. Mary stood very still, listening, nodding slightly, holding the phone tight with both hands, her shoulders hunched as if she were out in cold weather.

"Mary," he said.

Nothing.

He went into their bedroom and closed the door. The light coming through the windows was soft gold, and the room was deepening with shadows. He moved to the bed and sat down, and in a moment he noticed that he had begun a low sort of murmuring. He took a breath and tried to be still. From the other room, his wife's voice came to him. "Yes, I quite agree with you. But I'm just unable to put this . . ."

The voice trailed off. He waited. A few minutes later, she came to the door and knocked on it lightly, then opened it and looked in.

"What," he said.

"They're serious." She stood there in the doorway.

"Come here," he said.

She stepped to his side and eased herself down, and he moved to accommodate her. He put his arm around her, and then, because it was awkward, clearly an embarrassment to her, took it away. Neither of them could speak for a time. Everything they had been through during the course of deciding about each other seemed concentrated now. Ballinger breathed his wife's presence, the odor of earth and flowers, the outdoors.

"God," she said. "I'm positively numb. I don't know what to think."

"Let's have another baby," he said suddenly. "Melanie's baby will need a younger aunt or uncle."

Mary sighed a little forlorn laugh, then was silent.

"Did you tell her about us?" he asked.

"No," she said. "I didn't get the chance. And I don't know that I could have."

"I don't suppose it's going to matter much to her."

"Oh, don't say that. You can't mean that."

The telephone on the bedstand rang, and startled them both. He reached for it, held the handset toward her.

"Hello," she said. Then: "Oh. Hi. Yes, well, here." She gave it back to him.

"Hello," he said.

Melanie's voice, tearful and angry: "You had something you said you had to tell *me*." She sobbed, then coughed. "Well?"

"It was nothing, honey. I don't even remember—"

"Well, I want you to know I would've been better than you were, Daddy, no matter how hard it was. I would've kept myself from reacting."

"Yes," he said. "I'm sure you would have."

"I'm going to hang up. And I guess I'll let you know later if we're coming at all. If it wasn't for Mom, we wouldn't be."

"We'll talk," he told her. "We'll work on it. Honey, you both have to give us a little time."

"There's nothing to work on as far as William and I are concerned."

"Of course there are things to work on. Every marriage—" His voice had caught. He took a breath. "In every marriage there are things to work on."

"I know what I know," she said.

"Well," said Ballinger. "That's—that's as it should be at your age, darling."

"Goodbye," she said. "I can't say any more."

"I understand," Ballinger said. When the line clicked, he held the handset in his lap for a moment. Mary was sitting there at his side, perfectly still.

"Well," he said. "I couldn't tell her." He put the handset back in its cradle. "God. A sixty-three-year-old son-in-law."

"It's happened before." She put her hand on his shoulder,

then took it away. "I'm so frightened for her. But she says it's what she wants."

"Hell, Mary. You know what this is. The son of a bitch was her goddam teacher."

"Listen to you—what are you saying about her? Listen to what you're saying about her. That's our daughter you're talking about. You might at least try to give her the credit of assuming that she's aware of what she's doing."

They said nothing for a few moments.

"Who knows," Ballinger's wife said. "Maybe they'll be happy for a time."

He'd heard the note of sorrow in her voice, and thought he knew what she was thinking; then he was certain that he knew. He sat there remembering, like Mary, their early happiness, that ease and simplicity, and briefly he was in another house, other rooms, and he saw the toddler that Melanie had been, trailing through slanting light in a brown hallway, draped in gowns she had fashioned from her mother's clothes. He did not know why that particular image should have come to him out of the flow of years, but for a fierce minute it was uncannily near him in the breathing silence; it went over him like a palpable something on his skin, then was gone. The ache which remained stopped him for a moment. He looked at his wife, but she had averted her eyes, her hands running absently over the faded denim cloth of her lap. Finally she stood. "Well," she sighed, going away. "Work to do."

"Mary?" he said, low; but she hadn't heard him. She was already out the doorway and into the hall, moving toward the kitchen. He reached over and turned the lamp on by the bed, and then lay down. It was so quiet here. Dark was coming to the windows. On the wall there were pictures; shadows, shapes, silently clamoring for his gaze. He shut his eyes, listened to the small sounds she made in the kitchen, arranging her flowers, running the tap. *Mary,* he had said. But he could not imagine what he might have found to say if his voice had reached her.

High-Heeled Shoe

Dornberg, out for a walk in the fields behind his house one morning, found a black high-heeled shoe near the path leading down to the neighboring pond. The shoe had scuffed places on its shiny surface and caked mud adhering to it, but he could tell from the feel of the soft leather that it was well made, the kind a woman who has money might wear. He held it in his hand and observed that his sense of equilibrium shifted; he caught himself thinking of misfortune, failure, scandal.

The field around him was peaceful, rife with the fragrances of spring. The morning sun was warm, the air dry, the sky blue. Intermittently, drowsily, the cawing of crows sounded somewhere in the distance, above the languid murmur of little breezes in the trees bordering the far side of the pond. A beautiful, innocent morning, and here he stood, holding the shoe close to his chest in the defensive, wary posture of the guilty—the attitude of someone caught with the goods—nervously scraping the dried mud from the shoe's scalloped sides.

The mud turned to dust and made a small red cloud about his head, and when the wind blew, the glitter of dust swept over him. He used his shirttail to wipe his face, then walked a few paces, automatically looking for the shoe's mate. He thought he saw something in the tall grass at the edge of the pond, but when he got to it, stepping in mud and catching himself on thorns to make his way, he found the dark, broken curve of a beer bottle. The owner of the pond had moved last fall to Alaska, and there were signs posted all over about the penalties for trespassing, but no one paid any attention to them. Casual littering went on. It was distressing. Dornberg bent down and picked up the shard of glass. Then he put his hand inside the shoe and stretched the leather, holding it up in the brightness.

He felt weirdly dislodged from himself.

Beyond the pond and its row of trees, four new houses were being built. Often the construction crews, made up mostly of young men, came to the pond to eat their box lunches and, sometimes, to fish. On several occasions they had remained at the site long after the sun went down; the lights in the most nearly finished house burned; other cars pulled in, little rumbling sports cars and shiny sedans, motorcycles, even a taxi now and again. There were parties that went on into the early morning hours. Dornberg had heard music, voices, the laughter of women, all of which depressed him, as though this jazzy, uncomplicated gaiety—the kind that had no cost and generated no guilt—had chosen these others over him. The first time he heard it, he was standing at the side of his house, near midnight, having decided to haul the day's garbage out before going to bed (how his life had lately turned upon fugitive urges to cleanse and purge and make order!). The music stopped him in the middle of his vaguely palliative task, and he listened, wondering, thinking his senses were deceiving him: a party out in the dark, as if the sound of it were drifting down out of the stars.

Some nights when sleep wouldn't come, he had stared out his window at the faint shadows of the unfinished houses and, finding the one house with all its windows lighted, had quietly made his way downstairs to the back door and stood in the chilly open frame, listening for the music, those pretty female voices—the tumult of the reckless, happy young.

TODAY, A SATURDAY, he carried what he had found back to his own recently finished house (some of the men on the construction crew were in fact familiar to him, being subcontractors who worked all the new houses in the area). The piece of glass he dropped in the trash can by the garage door, and the shoe he brought into the house with him, stopping in the little coat porch to take off his muddy boots.

His wife, Mae, was up and working in the kitchen, still wearing her nightgown, robe, and slippers. Without the use of dyes or rinses, and at nearly forty-seven years of age, her hair retained that rich straw color of some blondes, with a bloom of light brown in it. She'd carelessly brushed it up over her ears and tied it in an absurd ponytail which stood out of the exact middle of the back of her head. She was scouring the counter with a soapy dishcloth. Behind her, water ran in the sink. She hadn't seen him, and as he had done often enough lately, he took the opportunity to watch her.

This furtive attention, this form of secret vigilance, had arisen out of the need to be as certain as possible about predicting her moods, to be ready for any variations or inconsistencies of habit—teaching himself to anticipate changes. For the better part of a year, everything in his life with her had been shaded with this compunction, and while the reasons for it were over (he had ended it only this week), he still felt the need to be ever more observant, ever more protective of what he had so recently allowed to come under the pall of doubt and uncertainty.

So he watched her for a time.

It seemed to him that in passages like this—work in the house or in the yard, or even in her job at the computer store—her face gleamed with a particular domestic heat. Curiously, the sense of purpose, the intention to accomplish practical tasks, made her skin take on a translucent quality, as though these matters required a separate form of exertion, subjecting the sweat glands to different stimuli.

She saw him now and stepped away from the counter, which shined.

"Look at this." He held up the shoe.

She stared.

"I found it out by the pond." Somehow, one had to try to remember the kind of thing one would have done before everything changed; one had to try to keep the old habits and propensities intact.

"Whose is it?" she asked him.

"Someone in a hurry," he said, turning the shoe in his hand.

"Well, I certainly don't want it."

"No," he said. "Just thought it was odd."

"Somebody threw it away, right?"

"You wonder where it's been."

"What do these girls do to be able to drive those fancy foreign jobs, anyway?"

"The daughters of our landed neighbors."

"Playing around with the workforce."

"Maybe it's encouraged," he said.

"Are you okay?" she asked.

The question made him want to get outside in the open again. "Sure. Why?"

"It's odd," she said. "A high-heeled shoe. You look a bit flustered."

"Well, honey, I thought a shoe, lying out in the back—I thought it *was* odd. That's why I brought it in."

"Whatever you say." She had started back to work on the kitchen.

Again, he watched her for a moment.

"What," she said. "You're not imagining something awful, are you? I'll bet you looked around for a body, didn't you."

"Don't be absurd," he said.

"Well, I thought of it. I've become as morbid as you are, I guess."

"I'll get busy on the yard," he said.

"You sure you're okay?"

He tried for teasing exasperation: "Mae."

She shrugged. "Just asking."

WAS IT GOING TO BE IMPOSSIBLE, now that everything was over, now that he had decided against further risk, to keep from making these tiny slips of tone and stance? At times he had wondered if he were not looking for a way to confess: Darling, I've wronged you. For the past nine months I've been carrying on with someone at work—lunch hours, afternoon appointments, that trip to Boston (she met me there), those restless weekend days when I went out to a matinee (the motels in town have satellite movies which are still playing in the theaters). Oh, my darling, I have lavished such care on the problem of keeping it all from you that it has become necessary to tell you about it, out of the sheer pressure of our old intimacy.

Outside, he put the shoe in the trash, then retrieved it and set it on the wooden sill inside the garage. He would throw it away when it was not charged with the sense of recent possession, a kind of muted strife: he could not shake the feeling that the wearer of the shoe had not parted with it easily. He felt eerily proprietary toward it, as though any minute a woman might walk down the street in the disarming, faintly comical limp of a person bereft of one shoe, and ask him if he had its mate. He conjured the face: bruised perhaps, smeared and drawn, someone in the middle of the complications of passion, needing to account for everything.

THEY HAD BEEN MARRIED more than twenty-five years, and the children—two of them—were gone: Cecily was married and living in New York, and Todd was in his first year of college out in Arizona. Cecily had finished a degree in accounting, and was putting her husband through business school at Columbia. They were planners, as Dornberg's wife put it. When the schooling was over, they would travel, and when the travel was done, they'd think about having children. Everything would follow their carefully worked-out plan. She did not mean it as a criticism, particularly; it was just an observation.

"I have the hardest time imagining them making love," she'd said once.

This was a disconcerting surprise to Dornberg. "You mean you try to imagine them?"

"I just mean it rhetorically," she said. "In the abstract. I don't see Cecily."

"Why think of it at all?"

"I didn't say I dwelled on it."

He let it alone, not wanting to press.

"Come here," she said. "Let's dwell on each other a little."

The hardest thing during the months of what he now thought of as his trouble was receiving her cheerful, trustful affection, her comfortable use of their habitual endearments, their pet names for each other, their customary tenderness and gestures of attachment. He wondered how others bore such guilt: each caressive phrase pierced him, each casual assumption of his fidelity and his interest made him miserable, and the effort of hiding his misery exhausted him.

The other woman was the kind no one would suppose him to be moved by. Even her name, Edith, seemed far from him. Brassy and loud in a nearly obnoxious way, she wore too much makeup and her brisk, sweeping gestures seemed always to be accompanied by the chatter of the many bracelets on her bony wrists. She had fiery red hair and dark blue, slightly crossed eyes—the tiny increment of difference made her somehow more attractive—and she had begun things by stating bluntly that she wanted to have an affair with him. The whole thing had been like a sort of banter, except that she had indicated, with a touch to his hip, that she was serious enough. It thrilled him. He couldn't catch his breath for a few moments, and before he spoke again, she said, "Think it over."

This was months before the first time they made love. They saw each other often in the hallways of the courthouse, where he worked as an officer on custody cases (he had seen every permutation of marital failure, all the catastrophes of divorce) and she was a secretary in the law library. They started looking for each other in the downstairs cafeteria during coffee breaks and lunch hours, and they became part of a regular group of people who congregated in the smoking lounge in the afternoons. Everyone teased and flirted, everyone seemed younger than he, more at ease, and when she was with him, he felt the gap between him and these others grow narrower. Her voice and manner, her easy affection, enveloped him, and he felt as though he moved eloquently under the glow of her approval.

Of course, he had an awareness of the aspects of vulgarity surrounding the whole affair, its essential banality, having come as it did out of the fact that over the past couple of years he had been suffering from a general malaise, and perhaps he was bearing middle age rather badly: there had been episodes of anxiety and sleeplessness, several bouts of hypochondria and depression, and a steady increase in his old propensity toward gloom. This was something she had actually teased him about, and he had marveled at how much she knew about him, how exactly right she was to chide him. Yet even in the unseemly, forsaken-feeling last days and hours of his involvement with her, there remained the simple reprehensible truth that for a time his life had seemed somehow brighter—charged and brilliant under the dark blue gaze she bestowed on him, the look of appreciation. Even, he thought, of a kind of solace, for she *was* sympathetic, and she accepted things about his recent moods that only irritated Mae.

Perhaps he had seen everything coming.

ONCE, THEY STOOD TALKING for more than an hour in the parking lot outside the courthouse, she leaning on her folded arms in the open door of her small blue sports car, he with the backs of his thighs against the shining fender of someone's Cadillac. He had gone home to explain his lateness to Mae, feeling as he lied about being detained in his office the first real pangs of guilt, along with a certain delicious sense of being on the brink of a new, thrilling experience.

The affair commenced less than a week later. They went in her car to a motel outside the city. The motel was off the main road, an old establishment with a line of rooms like a stopped train—a row of sleeper cars. She paid for the room (she was single and had no accounts to explain to anyone), and for a while they sat on opposing beds and looked at each other.

"You sure you want to do this?" she said.

"No." He could barely breathe. "I've never done anything like this before."

"Oh, come on," she said.

"I haven't," he told her. "I've been a good husband for twenty-five years. I love my wife."

"Why are you here, then?"

"Sex," he said. "I can't stop thinking of you."

She smiled. "That's what I like about you. You're so straight with me."

"I'm scared," he said.

"Everybody is," she told him, removing her blouse. "Except the stupid and the insane."

There was a moment, just as they moved together, when he thought of Mae. He looked at the shadow of his own head on the sheet, through the silky, wrong-colored strands of her hair, and the room spun, seemed about to lift out of itself. Perhaps he was dying. But then she was uttering his name, and her sheer difference from Mae, her quick, bumptious energy and the strange, unrhythmical otherness of her there in the bed with him—wide hips and ruddiness, bone and breath and tongue and smell—obliterated thinking.

Later, lying on her side gazing at him, she traced the line of his jaw. "No guilt," she said.

"No."

"I love to look at you, you know it?"

"Me?"

"I like it that the pupils of your eyes don't touch the bottom lids. And you have long eyelashes."

He felt handsome. He was aware of his own face as being supple and strong and good to look at in her eyes.

Not an hour after this, seeing his own reflection in the bathroom mirror, he was astonished to find only himself, the same plain, middle-aged face.

SATURDAY WAS THE DAY for household maintenance and upkeep. The day for errands. While he ran the mower, hauling and pushing it back and forth in the rows of blowing grass, he felt pacified somehow. He had forgotten the shoe, or he wasn't thinking about it. He knew Mae was inside, and he could predict with some accuracy what room she would be working in. Between loads of laundry, she would run the vacuum, mop the floors, and dust the furniture and knickknacks—every room in the house. Toward the middle of the morning, she would begin to prepare something for lunch. This had been the routine for all the years since the children left, and as he worked in the shaded earth which lined the front porch, digging the stalks of dead weeds out and tossing them into the field beyond the driveway, he entertained the idea that his vulnerability to the affair might be attributed in some way to the exodus of the children; he had felt so bereft in those first weeks and months of their absence.

But then, so had Mae.

He carried a bag of weeds and overturned sod down to the edge of the pond and dumped it, then spread the pile with his foot. Somewhere nearby was the *tunk tunk* of a frog in the dry knifegrass. The world kept insisting on itself.

She called him in to lunch. He crossed the field, and she waited for him on the back deck, wearing faded jeans and a light pullover, looking, in the brightness, quite flawlessly young—someone who had done nothing wrong.

"Find another shoe?" she asked him.

He shook his head. "Got rid of some weeds. It's such a pretty day."

"Why did you save the other one?"

He walked up on the deck, kicking the edge of the steps to get dried mud from his boots. "I guess I did save it."

"It was the first thing I saw when I went through the garage to put the garbage out."

"I don't know," he said.

The breeze had taken her hair and swept it across her face. She brushed at it, then opened the door for him. "You seem so unhappy. Is there something going on at work?"

"What would be going on at work? I'm not unhappy."

"Okay," she said, and her tone was decisive. She would say no more about it.

He said, "It just seemed strange to throw the thing away."

"One of the workmen probably left it," she said. "Or one of their girlfriends."

The kitchen smelled of dough. She had decided to make bread, had spent the morning doing that. In the living room, which he could see from the back door, were the magazines and newspapers of yesterday afternoon. The shirt he had taken off last night was still draped over the chair in the hall-way leading into the bedroom. He suddenly felt very light-hearted and confident. He turned to her, reached over and touched her cheek. "Hey," he said.

She said, "What."

"Let's make love."

"Darling," she said.

THEY LAY QUIET in the stripe of shadow which fell across the bed. During their lovemaking he had felt a chill at his back, and as he'd often romantically strived to do when he was younger, he tried to empty his mind of anything but her physical being—the texture of her skin, the contours of her body, the faint lavender-soaped smell of her; her familiar lovely breathing presence. But his mind presented him with an image of the other woman, and finally he was lost, sinking, hearing his wife's murmuring voice, holding her in the shivering premonition of disaster, looking blindly at the room beyond the curve of the bed, as though it were the prospect one saw from high bluffs, the sheer edge of a cliff.

"Sweet," she said.

He couldn't speak. He lay back and sighed, hoping she took the sound as an indication of his pleasure in her. Part of him understood that this was all the result of having put the affair behind him; it was what he must weather to survive.

"Cecily called while you were weeding," she said.

He waited.

"I wanted to call you in, but she said not to."

"Is anything wrong?"

"Well," his wife said, "a little, yes."

He waited again.

She sighed. "She didn't want me to say anything to you."

"Then," he said, "maybe you shouldn't."

This made her turn to him, propping herself on one elbow. "We always tell each other everything."

He could not see through the cloudy, lighter green of her eyes in this light. Her questioning face revealed nothing.

"Don't we?" she said.

"We do."

She put one hand in his hair, combed the fingers through. "Cecily's afraid Will has a girlfriend at school. Well, he has a friend at school that Cecily's worried about. You know, they have more in common, all that."

"Do you think it's serious?" he managed.

"It's serious enough for her to worry about it, I guess. I told her not to."

He stared at the ceiling, with its constellations of varying light and shadow.

"Will's too single-minded to do any carrying on," she said. "He probably doesn't even know the other girl notices him."

"Is that what you told Cecily?"

"Something like that."

"Did you tell her to talk to Will about it?"

"Lord, no."

"I would've told her to talk to him."

"And put ideas in his head?"

"You don't mean that, Mae."

"I guess not. But there's no sense calling attention to it."

"I don't know," he said.

"It's not as if he's saving old shoes or anything."

"What?"

She patted his chest. "Just kidding you."

"IS IT SUCH AN ODD THING, putting that shoe in the garage?" he said.

They were in the kitchen, sitting at the table with the day's newspaper open before them. She had been working the crossword puzzle. The light of early afternoon shone in her newly brushed and pinned-back hair.

"Well?" he said.

She only glanced at him. "I was teasing you."

He got up and went out to the garage, took the shoe down from its place on the sill, and carried it to the garbage cans at the side of the house. The air was cooler here, out of the sun, like a pocket of the long winter. He put the shoe in the can and closed it, then returned to the kitchen. She hadn't moved from where she sat, still looking at the puzzle.

"I threw it away," he said.

Again, her eyes only grazed him. "Threw what away?"

"The shoe."

She stared. "What?"

"I threw the shoe away."

"I was just teasing you," she said, and a shadow seemed to cross her face.

He took his part of the paper into the living room. But he couldn't concentrate. The clock ticked on the mantel, the house creaked in the stirring breezes. Feeling unreasonably ill-tempered, he went back into the kitchen, where he brought the feather duster out of the pantry.

"What're you doing?" she said.

"I'm restless."

"Is it what I told you about Cecily?"

"Of course not." He felt the need to be forceful.

She shrugged and went back to her puzzle.

"Is something bothering you?" he asked.

She didn't even look up. "What would be bothering me?"

"Cecily."

"I told her it was nothing."

"You believe that?"

"Sure. I wouldn't *lie* to her."

In the living room, he dusted the surfaces, feathered

across the polished wood of the mantel and along the gilt or black edges of photographs in their frames: his children in some uncannily recent-feeling summer of their growing up, posing arm in arm and facing into the sunlight; his own parents staring out from the shade of a porch in the country fifty years ago; Mae waving from the stern of a rented boat. When he was finished, he set the duster on the coffee table and lay back on the sofa. Could he have imagined that she was hinting at him? He heard her moving around in the other room, opening the refrigerator, pouring something.

"Want some milk?" she called.

"No, thanks," he called back.

"Sure?"

"Mae. I said no thanks."

She stood in the arched entrance to the room and regarded him. "I don't suppose your restlessness would take you to the dining room and family room as well."

"No," he said.

"Too bad."

When she started out, he said, "Where're you going?"

"I'm going to lie down and read awhile. Unless you have other ideas."

"Like what?" he said.

"I don't know. A movie?"

"I don't feel like it," he told her.

"Well, you said you were restless."

He could think of nothing to say. And it seemed to him that he'd caught something like a challenge in her gaze.

But then she yawned. "I'll probably fall asleep."

"I might go ahead and get the other rooms," he offered.

"Let it wait," she said, her voice perfectly friendly, perfectly without nuance. "Let's be lazy today."

HE HAD ENDED THE AFFAIR with little more than a hint; that was all it had taken. The always nervy and apparently blithe Edith had nevertheless more than once voiced a horror of being anyone's regret or burden, was highly conscious of what others thought about her, and while she obviously didn't mind being involved with a married man, didn't mind having others know this fact, she would go to lengths not to be seen in the light of a changed circumstance: the woman whose passion has begun to make her an object of embarrassment.

The hint he had dropped was only a plain expression of the complications he was living with. It happened without premeditation one afternoon following a quick, chaste tussle in the partly enclosed entrance of an out-of-business clothing store in the city. They'd had lunch with five other people, and had stayed behind to eat the restaurant's touted coffee cake. They were casually strolling in the direction of the courthouse when the opportunity of the store entrance presented itself, and they ducked out of sight of the rest of the street, embracing and kissing and looking out at the row of buildings opposite, feeling how impossible things were: they couldn't get a room anywhere now, there wasn't time. They stood apart, in the duress of knowing they would have to compose themselves. The roofs of the buildings were starkly defined by gray scudding clouds—the tattered beginning of a storm.

"It's getting so I feel like I can't keep up," he said.

Her eyes fixed him in their blue depths. "You're not talking about you and Mae, are you."

"I don't know what I'm talking about."

"Sure you do," she said. Then she took his hands. "Listen, it was fun. It was a fling. It never meant more than that."

"I don't understand," he told her.

Edith smiled. It was a harsh, knowing smile, the look of someone who knows she's divined the truth. "I think we both understand," she said. Then she let go of him and walked out into the increasing rain.

Two days later she took another job, at one of the district courts far out in the suburbs; she told everyone they knew that she had wanted out of the city for a long time, and indeed it turned out that her application to the new job was an old one, predating the affair. The opportunity had arisen, and she'd been thinking about it for weeks. This came out at the office party to bid her farewell. He stood with her and all the others, and wished her the best of luck. They were adults, and could accept and respect each other; it was as if everything that had happened between them was erased forever. They shook hands as the celebrating died down, and she put her arms around his neck, joking, calling him sexy.

THE DARK WAS COMING LATER EACH NIGHT.

He went out on the deck and watched the sky turn to shades of violet and crimson, and behind him Mae had begun to prepare dinner. There were lights on in the other house. Two cars had pulled up. Dornberg heard music. As he watched, a pair drove up on a motorcycle—all roaring, dust-blown, the riders looking grafted to the machine like some sort of future species, with an insectile sheen about them, and a facelessness: the nylon tights and the polished black helmets through which no human features could be seen.

When the motorcycle stopped, one rider got off, a woman—Dornberg could tell by the curve of the hips—who removed her helmet, shook her hair loose and cursed, then stalked off into the light of the half-finished porch, holding the helmet under her arm like a football. Her companion followed, still wearing his helmet.

Inside Dornberg's house, Mae made a sound, something like an exhalation that ended on a word. He turned, saw that she was standing in the entrance of the living room, in the glow of the television, gesturing to him.

"What?" he said, moving to the screen door.

"Speaking of your high-heeled shoe. Look at this."

He went in to her. On television, a newsman with an over-bright red tie was talking about the body of a woman that had been found in a pile of leaves and mud in a wooded section of the county. Dornberg listened to the serious, steady, reasonable news voice talking of murder. The picture cut away and the screen was blank for an instant, and when he heard the voice pronounce the name Edith before going on to say another last name, the name of some other girl, his heartbeat faltered. On the screen now was a photograph of this unfortunate woman, this coincidence, not *his* Edith, some poor stranger, twenty-five years old, wearing a ski sweater, a bright, college-picture smile, and brown hair framing a tanned face. But the moment had shocked him, and the shock was still traveling along the nerves in his skin as Mae spoke. "You don't suppose—"

"No," he said, before he could think. "It's not her."

His wife stared at him. He saw her out of the corner of his eye as he watched the unfolding story of the body that was in tennis shoes and jeans—the tennis shoes and part of a denim cuff showing as men gently laid it down in a fold of black plastic.

"Tennis shoes," he managed. But his voice caught.

She still stared at him. On the screen, the newsman exuded professional sincerity, wide-eyed, half frowning. Behind him, in a riot of primary colors and with cartoonish exaggeration, was the representation of a human hand holding a pistol, firing.

Mae walked into the kitchen.

He called after her. "Need help?"

She didn't answer. He waited a moment, trying to decide how he should proceed. The damage done, the television had shifted again, showing beer being poured into an iced glass in light that gave it impossibly alluring hues of amber and gold. Already the world of pure sensation and amusement had moved on to something else. He switched the TV off, some part of him imagining, as always, that it went off all over the country when he did so.

In the kitchen, she had got last night's pasta out, and was breaking up a head of lettuce.

"What should I do?" he asked, meaning to be helpful about dinner, but he was immediately aware of the other context for these words. "Should I set the table?" he added quickly.

"Oh," she said, glancing at him. "It's fine." The look she had given him was almost shy; it veered from him and he saw that her hands shook.

He stepped to the open back door. By accident, then, she knew. All the months of secrecy were done. And he could seek forgiveness. When he understood this, his own guilty elation closed his throat and made it difficult to speak. Outside, in the dusk beyond the edge of the field, from the lighted half-finished house, the sound of guitar music came.

"Think I'll go out on the deck," he told her.

"I'll call you when it's ready." Her voice was precariously even, barely controlled.

"Honey," he said.

"I'll call you."

"Mae."

She stopped. She was simply standing there, head bowed, disappointment and sorrow in the set of her jaw, the weary slope of her shoulders, waiting for him to go on. And once more he was watching her, this person who had come all the long way with him from his youth, and who knew him well enough to understand that he had broken their oldest promise to each other—not the one to be faithful so much as the one to honor and protect, for he had let it slip, and he had felt the elation of being free of the burden of it. It came to him then: the whole day had been somehow the result of his guilty need to unburden himself, starting with the high-heeled shoe. And there was nothing to say. Nothing else to tell her, nothing to soothe or explain, deflect or bring her closer. In his mind the days ahead stretched into vistas of quiet. Perhaps she might even decide to leave him.

"What are you thinking?" he managed to ask.

She shrugged. Nothing he might find to say in this moment would be anything he could honestly expect her to believe.

"Are you okay?" he said.

Now she did look at him. "Yes."

"I'll be out here."

She didn't answer.

He stepped out. The moon was rising, a great red disk

above the trees and the pond. A steady, fragrant breeze blew, cool as the touch of metal on his cheek. The music had stopped from the other house, though the lights still burned in the windows. Behind him, only slightly more emphatic than usual, was the small clatter of plates and silverware being placed. He watched the other house for a while, in a kind of pause, a stillness, a zone of inner silence, like the nullity of shock. Yet there was no denying the stubborn sense of deliverance which breathed through him.

When something shattered in the kitchen, he turned and saw her walk out of the room. He waited a moment, then quietly stepped inside. She had broken a wine glass; it was lying in pieces on the counter where it had fallen. He put the smaller pieces into the cupped largest one and set it down in the trash, then made his way upstairs and along the hall toward the bedroom. He went slowly. There seemed an oddly tranquilizing aspect about motion itself. It was as if he were being pulled back from disaster by the simple force of sensible actions: cleaning up broken glass, climbing stairs, mincing along a dimly lighted hallway.

She had turned the blankets back on the bed but was sitting at her dressing table, brushing her hair.

"Aren't you going to eat?" he said.

"I broke one of the good wine glasses."

"I'm not hungry either," he told her.

She said nothing.

"Mae. Do you want to talk about it?"

Without looking at him, she said, "Talk about what?"

He waited.

"We only have two left," she said. "I just hate to see the old ones get broken."

"Never again," he said. "I swear to you."

"It happens," she told him. "And it's always the heirlooms."

"How long have you known?" he said.

"Known?"

Again, he waited.

"You've been so strange all day. What're you talking about?"

He understood now that the burden had been returned to him, and he was not going to be allowed to let it slip.

"I guess I'll go back down and watch some television," he said.

She kept brushing her hair.

Downstairs, he put the uneaten dinner away, then turned the television on and stood for a minute in the uproar of voices and music—a huge chorus of people singing about a bank. Finally he walked out on the deck again. From the unfinished house came the hyperbolic percussion of an electronic synthesizer. Shadows danced in the windows, people in the uncomplicated hour of deciding on one another. A moment later, he realized that Mae had come back downstairs. She was standing in the kitchen in her bathrobe, pouring herself a glass of water. She glanced at him, glanced in his direction; he was uncertain if she could see him where he stood. She did not look unhappy or particularly distressed; her demeanor was somehow practical, as though she had just completed an unpleasant task, a thing that had required effort but was finished, behind her. Seeing this sent a little thrill of fear through him, and then he was simply admiring her in that light that was so familiar, the woman of this house, at evening.

Quietly, feeling the need, for some reason, to hurry, he

stepped down into the grass and walked out of the border of the light, toward the pond. He did not go far, but stood very still, facing the column of shimmering moonlight on the water and the four bright, curtainless windows in that house where the music grew louder and louder. He no longer quite heard it. Though the whole vast bowl of the night seemed to reverberate with drums and horns, he was aware only of the silence behind him, listening for some sound of his wife's attention, hoping that she might call him, say his name, remind him, draw him back to her from the darkness.

A NOTE ON THE TYPE

The principal text of this
Modern Library edition was set in Fairfield,
the first typeface from the hand of the distinguished
American artist and engraver Rudolph Ruzicka (1883–1978).
In its structure Fairfield displays the sober and sane qualities
of the master craftsman whose talent has long been dedicated
to clarity. It is this trait that accounts for the trim grace and
vigor, the spirited design and sensitive balance,
of this original typeface.

Rudolph Ruzicka was born in Bohemia and came to
America in 1894. He set up his own shop, devoted to wood
engraving and printing, in New York in 1913 after a varied
career working as a wood engraver, in photoengraving and
banknote printing plants, and as an art director and freelance
artist. He designed and illustrated many books and was the
creator of a considerable list of individual prints—wood
engravings, line engravings on copper, and aquatints.